ACHING JOYS

A FLICKERING LIGHT AT THE END OF THE TUNNEL

ARNI

ISBN 979-8-88849-365-6

A Few Words from the Author

This happens to be my very first affair with the world of writing

'Am not quite sure, but hope, it's your first creative encounter with the world of literature. It's perfectly adventurous dad. You challenged yourself wholeheartedly'. Remarked **Vinni**, my daughter, also the biggest critic of mine. She qualifies as my best friend too, without any doubt, whatsoever!

Vinni stirred me up from within. Somewhere down the line, she had discovered my underlying passion for writing. She knew my wistful desire for a creative work that has been lying inside me frozen and out of sight for a long time beneath the complexities of an ordinary life. She smartly explores it and with much ease, engaging me in some charming conversational techniques, delicately ignites the long-awaited spark and pulls it out with her bare hands!

In many different ways, she added grace and style to this silent start. No surprise, she is the first reader!

Heartfelt thanks to **Vaishnavi**. Without your magnanimous support and guidance, this work wouldn't have happened. You shared your precious guidance and expertise

Prime dedication to **Rajlakshmi**, my wife whom I fondly address Raja. She always thought I've it in me, but never bothered to pamper me acknowledging it with an open heart. Had she, I must've been boundlessly happy, to the peaks of the Blue sky. Yet, am delightful that she knew it before anyone else did!

Next, to all those young hearts who still cherish that aching, yet joyful boyhood memories, for they're the ones who I believe, despite being at the fag-end of their youthfulness, still wandering as a kid without a trace of beauty being lost in the long corridor of a stressful life

Aching Joys– If felt to the Reader, carries shadows of true events and experiences, it's not a mere coincidence. It may seem wild, scenic, and carefree too. A loosely-knitted replica of an unknown somebody's flesh and blood!

I've made an attempt to envisage the underlying feelings and emotions of little Sanju. This book gives the reader a thick insight into different frames of his life. No emotional respite, concluding with some needle-sharp question marks strewn around, eyeing Mothers...to a great extent!

Chapter 1

Sanjay, slackly sits in his rocking chair. He is too enervated, more mentally than physical. The chair is oscillating gently to and fro, and the strokes become weaker like the closing swings of a baby cradle before it stops. Rails of the chair make feeble knocks on the floor, almost the last ones. It's rhythmic, harmonious to his ears. No one knows it for sure whether he is awake or asleep

On a certain day, deep within, when your childhood re-appears and disturbingly opens up at a stage where your inner thought processes are caught between the young robust yesterday, which is dead and the not-yet-born tomorrow, that shall bring the shades of death knell of energy and exuberance, which are the marks of a youth, it's too painful!

Bhaskar who comes early morning to milk cows in the neighbourhood, sometimes hears the tuk-tuk sound of the chair, evident that Sanjay got up early than usual that day

However, when he wakes up at 5 or 6 in the morning, after the morning routine, he occupies the chair and slips into a dizzy mood as he has no more busy schedules. Sometimes, it looks like; he is wanting a second round of sleep in the chair as though his regular sleep quota was not enough. But in fact, gone the days are when Sanjay used to get sound sleep, till Seven or Eight in the morning

It's almost midnight. Uncharacteristically cool, breezy summer night. Sanjay left his bed long ago. Settles in his favourite rocking chair placed in the lattice. Sometimes, one can find him occupied in his chair as early as 3 or 4 in the morning

Today, he is in deep pensive thoughts. This happens to him quite often. Too many thoughts come galloping in. It's then, a whirlpool of haphazardly impulsive notions!

His subconscious mind opens and roughs him up. He gets carried away by those deep-routed emotions and feelings. His disorderly mind slowly opens like a parachute without his conscience

His mind flies back to his intense days spreading across adolescence and teens

My name is Sanjay. If you are one among those who went through warm and cheerful childhood memories, you may not find me charming and charismatic!

Scene transition

Little Sanju busy playing native ball game. His arch rival Ramesh at the other end. Friends cheer them making a semi-circle facing the water bodies

Sanjay is my real name, but conveniently trimmed by the folks around to a tiny version, Sanju. May be, because it's shorter by one alphabet and easy to pronounce. Almost everyone around lovingly calls me Sanju. Am popularly known as Sanju in my school as well. Anyway, am glad that Sanju sounds more cute and pretty rather than Sanjay, which sounds quite majestic though

Am a 9-year-old lanky, frail boy with pale and fence-sitting eyes. That's me, rolled-up in a capsule!

Sanju..Sanju..Amma calls asking to wind up the play

I see her on the road showing me weird signals of impatience

If am not wrong, Sanju is the name given by my mother who keeps claiming that it's my original name though there is no documented evidence to prove her claim. All my academic records and personal documents put it beyond doubt that my name is Sanjay

'Take this', I say without heeding to Amma's call, kicks the ball with my right upper foot to the other end

It's a very tough crude form of game. One hundred percent Desi. One needs to play this to understand the tricks. It's played one against one or in teams. Either way, this has been one of the fascinating games in my boyhood

Ramesh, he is a strong player, kicks it back with great force

'Oops..you are too good my friend, I must accept', I scream

Ramesh laughs aloud! My compliment goes well with him

I don't have too many friends. Am very choosy to befriend people. Ramesh is my oldest friend, also my fiercest rival in all sports and games

Other than him, tall and bubbly Udhay and thin-built Atchu. Atchu is slightly younger in our peer group. Suresh and his younger brother Sunil are my closest friends

Game in the peak with our spirits riding high

'Howzzat'? Ramesh kicks the ball back aiming at my boundary

Oh My God! This Ramesh is a real tough guy. I find it hard to contain him

'Am going to floor you today, Sanju'. He is taunting my previous day's defeat at his hands

I had no answer this time. I simply let the ball pass through my boundary, watching it helplessly, for his shot is too fast and powerful. Beyond my reach

He always has the desire to win stronger than the opponent

Am getting ready to go for a fresh service, having gone down 1 – 2. Game in the peak with our spirit further up and strong..

Sanju..Sanju..Sanju Amma's distress call. It's a dire warning, I know. If I don't pack up the game now, her cane is going to do all the talk

'Let's call it off for the day Ramesh', I say. My voice smothered in disappointment

'Your mother throws the spanner right in the middle. Never lets you play with friends. You don't finish it off. It takes our spirit away. It's disgusting Sanju'. He is annoyed at my half-way departure

I didn't reply. I've no choice other than run back home

'Will catch up tomorrow', I wave to Ramesh

'Am going to kill you with the ball tomorrow Ramesh'. I don't miss to warn my friend while rushing back home

'I've been alerting you since half an hour, you bloody brat. Can't you bloody pack up the stupid game when am calling? I'll bang your head if you repeat it, you filthy creature', Amma's heavy downpour

'Take this 1-rupee note and go to shop, and don't steal that 5 paisa commission for candy. I want the exact balance amount back. Go and wash your this structure first, you are looking like a monkey straight from the woods', Amma

I take water in a bucket and go near my pet Mulberry tree. I planted it a few years ago. Slowly cleansed my skinny physique while looking up the Mulberry branches. The tree has grown strong enough now. I can fix my swing in the first branch

Leaving for shop. It's almost 6pm and is feeling hungry. Had thought, Amma would give something to munch but that was not to be..

My empty stomach makes me further dull. Knees going week

Back home from the shop, it's quarter to 7, and it's time to take bath and get to studies

I finish an express bath. Trying to put my legs into the faded trunks, which had bull's eye at both buttock cheeks, but I had darned it using old unmatched cloth bits. It now looks like trunks with embroidered butts!

I sit for evening coffee; don't know why my elder sister Somi has a malicious smile on her lips. She looks at me

Her smile is annoying. Looks wicked

'What'? I ask Somi, who is2 years older than me. I still conveniently address her by name, no Didi business

'Nothing significant', she replies

'Then why such a stupid smile on your bloody face. Am I nude or what?' Am furious

'Slightly less than that. Now, you've the looks of a circus joker in these shorts. It's colourful from the back with the hollows still visible. As though enemy soldiers across the borders shot you exactly on your butts', she giggles

Am in no mood to enjoy her untimely funny discovery. Am hungry and tired

'Are you sleepy? It's only half past 7'. Granny's soft voice shakes me up

She crawls to me from the farthest corner. We sometimes find Granny changes her physical location from one to another without caring to get up. She says it's waste of time

'Not at all Granny, feel like gobble up something. This stupid is mocking at my trunks and making fun of me', I say pointing at Somi

'Don't worry my little darling', Granny caresses my not-so-thick hairs and pulls me closer to her

Granny loves me greater than anything else in the whole universe. She is close to Eighty Five years of age, but if anyone asks her age, she would say, 75. Granny never gets older beyond the 75 mark as her ageing clock seems to have stuck at this number since time immemorial. Maybe, she doesn't want to grow further old!

It's half past 8. I skip my homework and lie down flat on the floor. It's dinner time and the menu is not likely to boost my appetite. Rice and lemon pickle. Why doesn't Amma cook anything else for dinner? Am frustrated eating the same food daily night. May be Amma is frustrated too cooking the same stuff daily. I think, our menu never changes, just like the rules of Life Insurance Corporation of India. If the policy holder has a longer lifespan, LIC gains; otherwise, it's a jackpot to the nominee. Either way, rule hasn't changed since decades!

Am the youngest son among 3 siblings. Sister, Somi comes in the middle. I had a younger female sibling who had died of malnutrition and recurrent childhood illnesses. I've a clouded memory of her

Can't forget how my Appa's face looked that day. He was grim and impassive while carrying her coffin box on his shoulders

Profound grief writ all over his face

Only a father knows, how it feels when he carries the coffin of his child

No doubt, small coffins are the heaviest!

Don't know where the thoughts take me

I shut my eyes and stare into the dark. Granny sleeps still and silent. This is quite unusual of her. Somi snores rhythmically with exactly regular intervals

Scene transition

My Class Teacher, Ms. Ramani would suddenly shoot questions on regional literature or current affairs. Sometimes, not quite sure about the answer, we front-benchers raise our hands halfway making chorus, 'me.. me', mostly to impress the girls sitting opposite, the star attraction of our class. In fact, the root cause, why we boys make it to the class with that extra coat of talcum powder on our face, without a day break!

It's now annual exam time. Am in Class IV. Only an average student by any stretch. Maybe, selectively above average with typical desirables, say poem recital or short sprints in sports

Our Maths teacher and neighbour Ms. Ratchel writes questions on the wooden Black board. The stress of chalk piece is causing minor tremors to the thin board frame. Old triangular legs of the board somehow dare squeaking

I keep staring at the Blackboard from top to bottom without a wink

Oh My God! 10 questions! My heart pounds. Feel like run away from here

Slowly start some scribble on my slate with my cardamom-size slate pencil

My slate is 2 years old with the wooden frames hanging loose at 2 sides and 1 frame terribly missing. My slate is living dangerously with the help of only 1 frame!

I attempt all questions but could answer only a few, which I thought to be right. When I really do not understand even the questions, how can I answer them!

Wow! Finally, the horrifying exercise is over. I get the score. Teacher writes 9/25 in my slate in a magnified size. I don't understand what this mark means. Am I passed or failed? It's high mark or low mark? No courage to ask Ms. Ratchel

While running back home, I make some dramatic changes to the digits on my slate. I crop-up the number 9, which now looks like a different number, not sure exactly what, to confuse Amma at home

'What's this? I can't make out anything', Amma roars looking at the peculiar ancient civilization age digit on my slate, and throws the slate back to me. I resort to evading action like an acrobat and it flies and knocks down Amma's Westclox timepiece, eventually lands on the bed!

The number wholesomely looks like a piece of Modern Art! She is unable to figure it out. No wonder, she loses her cool

'Don't know', I simply answer

Time is quarter to 1. I run to kitchen looking for food

Chapter 2

Road network in our region is vertically steep due to geographical specifications. Very tiresome to walk 1km. Some part of roads looks like the chicken neck in India's map, but we children enjoy exploring those hostilities. Some other times, walk down fast with much ease since the road is descending

Our house has a frontage uneven gravel road. Not rolled, filled with rubbles and pits. It pains to walk without slippers. It's a luxury to have a pair of lightweight rubber footwear, which costs about 5 rupees. For children, the price is low since the size is small

I study at the Lower Primary school, which is at a walkable distance from my house. Am hungry after 5 hours of struggle in the class. Last session was Maths, which tore me apart. It's cold-blooded murder in the form of education!

Most of the children tend to run in the middle of a walk. Am no different. I rundown to my house. My slippers are almost worn out, but I don't care. Suddenly, I stumble upon a hard Red stone and fall hard on the ground. My nose and lips bleed. Scratches on my cheeks and a deep cut below right knee

I see my Amma busy in spicy talk with my aunt in my neighbourhood. This aunt is older to Appa. She is a widow ever since we see her. She is our only aunt whom we are in close acquaintance with since she lives very close to us with her son and daughter-in-law. She has a grandson too

Amma doesn't bother to lift her chin up and come and see me. Am in tears, limp, and exert myself to make it inside house. Don't know what to do

I take to a corner, weeping, when Amma comes in with a mosey gait. She doesn't seem to be worried

'Couldn't you walk carefully, why did you run, huh'? Amma rages on me without caring to have a look at my wounds

Am in distress and can't answer. Heartbroken to see my good pair of uniform torn and splashed with mud

'Have your food and wash your uniform. Don't attend the afternoon session', Amma orders

Obviously, there is no Appeal against her orders on me. But I don't want to take her order for the time-being

Here comes my Granny. Hopefully, she had a short visit to the neighbourhood. Got to know about the incident and rushes back home..

'What happened my child'? Granny sits near to me and fondly cleanses my wounds. She wipes the mud-stained blood from the wounds with the tip of her dhoti, glares at Amma

'Where were you? Why didn't you care for his wounds? How could you be so cruel to this small little boy'? Granny's voice pitching high

'Not interested. You take care', Amma replies casually and leaves the scene

'Let Bala come, we'll see', Granny refers to my Appa. 'I've no regards in the family. She could be a little more polite. Am her husband's mother, after all', Granny yells

Granny sits flat on the floor and stretches her legs straight, and keeps my head on her laps

She is my paternal grandmother. She has always been there with us ever since I can remember

I shut my eyes, gently slip into a nap. I always feel loved and cared when my Granny is around. She is filled with warmth and kindness. Am not feeling pain now. It's an extraordinary experience

Scene transition

Maths period, Standard V, A division. 'A' stands to denote English Medium. Am enrolled in a popular Seminary high school in our town. Elder brother Nakul bhaiya and sister Somi study in the same school

It's an August institution in our town in many respects. It's a renowned seminary high school located in the heart of the city. This school produces more sportstars than academically brilliant students. About 200mtrs away from the school, facing the main road, we can find one of the most famous colleges of the state, belongs to the same diocese. This school and college produced a number of stalwarts in sports and state administration

We are newly inducted into the English medium. The very first English medium batch of the school.

I curse myself. Had I not scored good marks in English in Class IV final exam, I wouldn't have been sandwiched between the trauma of learning a hostile language and the comforts of our plush regional language!

Our Headmistress Ms. Agnes says that it's an interestingly novel idea of having an English medium division in our school, which is otherwise a regional medium school. Am one among this coveted batch of 26!

There is another top class English medium school in the town, which the students of other schools envy. It produces cent percent result in Matric every year. From standard 1 to X, only English. Using regional language inside the campus is a big taboo here. We hear from our seniors that its students speak English as smooth as swallowing a favourite ice cream cone!

And here, this fancy language hurts me. I find it hard to get going. No comments on Maths! Day by day, this subject is becoming a thorn in my flesh. It's hurting too much!

'Open your homework notebook and read your answers', Maths Teacher Mr. Lucius Gabriel's rough loud noise echoes in the small class room. He is lean and tall, appears regularly in typical regional outfits. He is more than 6 feet tall with a scrawny physique. His lifeless eyes locate in deep manholes

My frail body starts shivering

'He is going to bang me today as well', am haunted

Ever since this academic year started, Mr. Lucius Gabriel has been really brutal. His tramp inside the classroom accompanied with intermittent swings of the cane in the air is enough to send shivers down my spine. When he takes those deadly steps towards me, I literally wet my trunks..

The on-going chapter is Fractions, and I do not understand even a fraction of Fractions!

The so-called bright frontline students stretch their forearm with elbows fixed on the desktop signalling their readiness to show their answers first. It's nothing new to me, for we too did the same in my previous school in Class IV. However, teacher may or may not pick that student to announce the answer

Alas! Am a frontbencher here too by default though I don't make the cut even to the average level. Am a frontbencher for all ironic reasons, which are going to give me constant bouts of struggle and turmoil in the long run. I get the signs and symptoms since the beginning of the session. Here, when frontbenchers lift their hand being ready with answers, I look at them as traitors, for Mr. Lucius Gabriel is going to hear to my answer if they fail to produce the right answer!

Mr. Lucius Gabriel is listening to the answers one by one, coming near to us from the Dias

It's now my turn. Oh My God!

With all the courage and strength of the universe mustered together, I simply open my homework note, the page is blank having not done the homework the previous day, and I simply whisper an illusionary answer

'Sir, 2/3'..

He looks bewildered, and in a jiffy, barges towards me as though I pricked his butt from behind with a nail clipper. He storms at me, and in one stroke, he snatches my book. The page's blank. His tiny eyes come out of the deep holes

'You little rascal, do you think am a clown'?

'I wasn't at home yesterday', conversations must be in English. This is Rule number 1 for us

'I didn't know how to..'I further fumble for words. Clumsy as am not sure about sentence formation

'Where in heaven's name have you been, you bloody cartoon'?

Am losing my balance and will fall down any time. The whole Class is watching me with renewed interest. Some of the boys and girls taunt and jest at me including the most charming girl, Rose whom all boys in the class have a secret crush on. Her smile brings together beauty and innocence with a halo of infectious traits at such a tender age!

I feel awfully bad at my own poster, especially, when Rose is watching

Can't blame them. They're in a frivolous mood

Mr. Lucius Gabriel loses his cool. No prior warning. He starts caning me Black and Blue...on my back, stomach, thighs, legs. I run for a shelter. If there's a pothole, I would have put my head inside and tried my luck. But there isn't any!

'Sir, please don't', am in tears

'Sir, No. Please stop', my best friend, Joyce jumps in for my help. He comes quickly into the middle and pleads

This annoys Mr. Lucius Gabriel further, but he isn't expressive of that..

Joyce is the elder son of our Class Teacher, Ms. Theresa. She teaches English

We sense that there exists a shade of jealous among the teaching faculty, which invariably reflects on their acts when they confront each other's children, like the one which Joyce is in now

Nothing could pacify Mr. Lucius Gabriel. He becomes a blood-thirsty demon

'You are an ass. You don't know Maths. You tricked me giving stupid imaginary answer. He hurls filthy words on me

'You bloody shit hole, trying to pull the wool over my eyes', Mr. Lucius Gabriel

He doesn't seem to stop any time soon

To a 10-year-old hapless boy, hailing from a mediocre background, Mr. Lucius Gabriel is the cruellest human being on planet Earth!

I start running from corner to corner to escape but he wouldn't stop. Finally, the cane takes the form of a broom, and he leaves me now..

My skin is ridden with bruises and blood clots all over

He didn't punish a student for a genuine cause. He shamed and abused a tender human life!

This day, I understand, am going to hate Maths forever. And my hatred is directly attributable to Mr. Lucius Gabriel, who is nothing but a beast!

As though a part of big charity, Mr. Lucius Gabriel allows me to go and wash my face

I step out. 'Hey you stop there', Joyce, perhaps my lone sympathizer in the class follows me

Am ashamed. Unable to stop and lock my eyes with him, still sobbing

'Hey, please don't mind Sanju. I didn't laugh when the whole class laughed at you, right'?

'Thankful to you Joyce', words scribble out of my mouth

'Don't worry man. I know, you are good in English, and you can floor anyone in the class in that subject. Hell with Maths', Joyce

It seems, he also hates Maths, or Mr. Lucius Gabriel But he's the son of our Class Teacher and is among the top students, overall. He sits next to me in the front bench and we are good friends by now

He would peep into my answer sheet during English class tests and I wouldn't mind him steal my answers

His words give me solace. When in distress, if there is one single person around to hold your pinky finger and lift up your spirits, it works wonders like the solitary traveller suddenly finds oasis in a desert. You can cling on to that and move on miles ahead!

'Am awaiting the upcoming English test', I say vigorously. 'I will show all those jokers who laughed at me when Mr. Lucius Gabriel was lashing me'

'You should pal. Am with you'. He pats my shoulder and offers me ice candy the next day

I return him with a joyous smile filled with thanks, and we both return to class

By this time, Maths period is over, and am hugely relieved

Here goes the long bell. Classes for the day come to an end

I run out first as if am running for my life escaping the clutches of a devil!

Chapter 3

Back from school

'Hi Granny', I rammed on to Granny pushing her down

Trying hard to conceal my teary swollen eyes from Granny

'You little rascal', she screams trying to get up. I hold her thin hands and wrench her up

She notices the bruises and bloody scratches on my entire body. Granny comes near and gently touches the marks all over my body. It's damn painful all over

Without being told a word, Granny understands what I went through in the school

I sob uncontrollably

'Here it's for you', she takes out a piece of bread from the upper fold of her dhoti and stretches to me

'Wow'! I grab it with a dive like a slip fielder taking an extraordinary catch in the cricket field

It's a thick slice. It's the top dense slice of a bread loaf, and she knows that portion of loaf tastes that extra bit and it's my favourite. Some brands we get here resemble the popular Texas toast texture wise

'Hmm..Yummy', I gobble it up as fast as I could

'Go and drink a glass of water, or else it may choke your throat', Granny warns

I can notice, her aged eyes are moist

I plant a soft kiss on her cheek, winking my right eye signalling everything is kay with me and nothing is too bothersome. But Granny reads my mind better than an expert psychologist

From time immemorial, I haven't seen her having teeth. That could be the reason, why her cheeks look hollow, like a vintage Codd-neck bottle

I run to the kitchen, gulp down a glass of water and remove my school uniform

I insert myself inside a pair of old cotton trunks and a sleeveless summer vest

'Where're mother and Somi, and how about Nakul bhaiya, I said

'Nobody is back home yet'

'Where's Amma'?

'I don't know', comes her lazy reply. Granny's nature is such. She doesn't want to speak about Amma. They both can't live cordially together under one roof. A classic example for mother-in-law vs. daughter-in-law, where both are typical Indians!

'Your sister will come cleaning the road all the way from school'

Granny is mockingly at Somi'sextra-long fashionably stitched uniform skirt. In Granny's opinion, Somi's skirt somewhat looks like a Hoop Petticoat without those extra frills. From the very first day she saw Somi in her skirt, Granny expressed her displeasure. Per Granny, girls shouldn't be too much fashionable, and must follow traditional walk of life in every respect. But Amma doesn't care a heck of it

Granny would taunt Somi, 'your skirt works like a multi-broom device when you walk'

'She is not good at studies as well', Granny adds up

'Leave it all Granny', I pinch her skinny cheeks

'By the way, what's at night'?

'You mean food'? Said Granny, as though she is not clear what I mean

'Ya, of course food, what else'?

'Let your mother come. She went to shop to buy groceries, may be back soon. It's already half past 5', Granny

'Why is she so late? Left my house at 3', again, Granny's soliloquy, while trying to lift herself up from the wooden block

I once more assist her get up

Scene transition

Sitting underneath my pet Mulberry tree on a piece of jute sack, I think am not visible to Amma in the dim street light, which is right in front of my house. The Teakwood light pole is mostly affected by termites. Bent hollow pipe with the Green-White round bulb shade almost surrendered to rust. Bulb holder is recently replaced with a new one, and that's somewhat the only glittering part in the whole assembly. Upper part of the street light structure formed the shaped of a fossil of an unknown ancient creature. The pole may any time kiss the ground and reduce to a pile of dust

Am crippled in horrifying thoughts. Can't really come to terms with what happened in the class today. It's simply barbaric at the part of Mr. Lucius Gabriel bashing me all over while am trying to escape like a prey clogged in the clutches of an eagle

He looks like Abraham Stoker's evil and monstrous character Dracula except those canine teeth. I run my fingers over the bruise marks

Our teaching faculty explains in English, and so, Mr. Lucius Gabriel. Am unable to conceive a damn bit about Maths. Except for English, Chemistry, and Arts & Sports, am struggling in all other subjects including regional language!

It was a nasty surprise to me when I failed in the recently concluded regional language class test. I achieved the biggest single digit number, and the subject teacher mocked at me..

'You, irritable migrant, can't fathom a tongue of your very own region? Disgusting, isn't it'?

Am aware, she goes a little too far in scolding me. But the student, who scored 9 out of 50 in his own regional language, has no moral right to open the mouth!

And perhaps, she also knows am bad at almost all subjects. The fact that am doing well in English doesn't impress her much, for she is a regional language specialist, and just for that single reason, she takes me as migrant, for whom the native tongue is like an alien language!

For her, am a migrant. I can hardly remember she called me Sanjay anytime

'Sanju, where're you my child'? Granny's voice abruptly brings me back to the present

Granny is too tired now-a-days. Gasps for breath sometimes, I can notice. She loves me so much that she can't take anyone bully me. She would never let anyone do any harm to me

But alas! She really has no control over Amma when she spanks me up

Those moments, Amma transforms into a mutant variant of a barbaric female human!

I spot Amma from a distance, 'hi Amma, why are you late'? I hold her hand

'Did you clean the house and fetch drinking water'? 'Where's Somi'? Amma

'She hasn't returned yet', I said in a dull voice, for am hungry and wanted something to eat. By the way, please note, am always hungry

I cleverly try to quit the scene, thinking to rescue myself from Amma's court orders. It's Amma's nature. If domestic chores are to be pushed and if Somi is not around, all the work loads fall on my shoulders by default.

And certainly, I can't dilly-dally any of her commands at any cost. Since, am the youngest little boy of the family, am vulnerable to a great extent. Am scared of Amma's cane. When she lifts it on me, she is ruthless. She picks up anything to bang on me when she is angry. Her caning leaves Reddish bruises and permanent scars on my little body everywhere

'Where're you scooting off'? Amma suddenly pulls me back

'Nowhere', my voice was feeble, showing absolute helplessness

'Get in and help me in cooking supper'

'Don't you want to eat something at night'? Amma asks rudely as though giving me food at night is a return gift for helping her push household chores

I go in, thinking of taking rice plates and cooking vessels for awash. Major part of our kitchen vessels are made up of Aluminium or Iron with White enamel coating. Similar stuff Tea mugs I see with some Army men. We've a limited stock of Stainless Steel plates too used exclusively for Nakul bhaiya and Appa

If you ask me who the VIP in my family is, it's undoubtedly Nakul bhaiya. At the age of nearly 15, he gets all the care and attention of Amma. Special food, special clothing, pocket money, and above all, total freedom to ramble around with friends. Lucky guy!

In a trice, our front door opens with a creaky noise, door hinges are rusted. Enters Somi. A readymade story written all over her face. She looks serious, and begins 'story telling' before being asked for being late

'Amma, do you know one thing'? 'I narrowly escaped from being hit by a fleeing taxi car'. The Ambassador taxi came very close to me, and Baby just pushed me aside, otherwise, I would have been in hospital. I escaped by a hair's breadth Amma', she concludes

Somi's goblet eyes almost come out of the eye orbits and fall on the floor. Baby is Uma aunt's daughter, our close neighbour

Somi has an uncanny knack of creating a story instantaneously. Just click the button, and she can start the narration. She makes even Sinbad, the fictional mariner proud in the blink of an eye

'Oh My God! Is it'? 'Come near, are you alright my Beti'? Amma curiously examines her all over as if she minutely escaped from something very tragic

Amma is very happy as her pet child had a providential escape though with her friend's timely indulgence!

Somi and Baby, both are ordinary in studies. Made for each other for many reasons. Both are allergic to text books and noticeably lethargic on school days. Baby though elder to me, is studying in regional medium parallel to my grade. She involves in senior level pranks and often invites the wrath of her teachers. Baby tops the list of Black-listed elements. Baby is a true example for indiscipline and disobedience personified

And by the way, this Baby is Somi's accidental companion whenever she gets back late from school!

I must probe into this tomorrow, I murmur

This night, I ought to help Amma in cooking and washing plates while Somi will have a luxurious recess

Amma orders me to fill the big containers also for storing water. Amma thinks that am the genie out of the bottle, and I can finish work one after another without break! She forgets that am an impoverished 10-year old!

After a pause, I come out to fetch water. Am thinking to do the dishes. I could see a mystifying smile on Somi's lips. She looks at me. It's pointless. She looks wicked. I really go nuts, and shout at her

'Don't show your 32. Am not interested seeing that'

'Don't care to take a look at my face', Somi retaliates

'What the hell is happening between the two? You tiny creature, go and do what I said, or else, no food for you', Amma at the top of her voice

I try to explain that Somi makes fun of me, but Amma in no mood to buy my running commentary. Amma has always been like that. My laments fall in deaf ears. None heeds to my small little grievances. No one understands that those small grievances are my real concerns, and could blow me away one day!

Am livid too. How could Amma be so blasé this often? She can lend me her ears at least once in a while. Am not the sinner all the time. She is judgemental!

'Go and get water in the mud pot, I must cook rice first, come on', Amma shakes me up

Amma uses earthen pots to cook rice and some special dishes. Granny says these pots are unglazed and free from toxic. And the food tastes great. Appa loves it most

'Sanju, where're you'? Amma storms out

Wow! Finally she takes my name. Am glad that my existence gets some esteem

I rush out; can't afford to test her patience any more

Scene transition

I plop myself down in my Granny's lap, curiously waiting to hear another story tonight. I hug her tight. She reciprocates with a pinch on my cheek and a smile. Ouch! Her nails are very hard..

It's a classic Granny smile wrapped with all the innocent beauty. When she bursts into a big laughter, the interior looks like a mystery cave hole with dark vacuum inside, partially showing her epiglottis with her trademark scent of betel leaf spreading out

Only to play a prank, I would take a toothbrush and ask, 'Is it yours Granny'?

She lifts her debilitated right hand and gestures to hit me, as though she is going to slap me seriously. Nevertheless, that is the only occasion she pretends to be angry on me

Her lap is the most restful place I could find in the entire world. It's where I eventually find peace and comfort, and rest my thin frame. Her laps is cosy and takes the shape of a convex couch when she sits with her folded knees straight up

She delivers a brand new story every night. All lovely stories, as pretty as a beautiful picture, laced with breathtakingly alluring situations. She has incredible narrative skill, which can make any script writer proud. She fabricates the whole story and makes it spicy and hot during romantic junctures. The all-time classic Raja & Rani story today, Dhobi's poor donkey the next day, a small slice from the fascinating Arabian tales comes next, chapters from Bhagvat Gita, episodes of Kurukshetra war, humiliation meted out to Karna, Karna's impactful role, Lord Krishna's advice to the great warrior Arjuna and so on. Stock never exhausts. Karna is my most favourite character among all warriors

Granny has a never ending rich collection of stories in her kitty, supplied anytime on my demand! She never disappoints me

If she could write, she would make an Albert Goodwin of her era, no surprise!

Scene transition

Close to midnight. Granny's another interesting bedtime story is long over. I couldn't sleep. Not sure whether my old mattress is itchy or the hurls I receive from Amma or the harrowing experience I had in the class today, unable to figure out the exact reason. Could be a horrible mix of all

The small little boy within me is traumatized. There are too many blanks!

'I should be confident and gel up with other boys in the Class', I whisper to myself. But the idea fizzles out, for I literally have only a few friends in the Class or in the whole school sans Joyce or may be in the whole world!

'Aren't you asleep my child'? Granny's stammering voice disconnects me from my intrusive thoughts

'Unable to sleep', I say

'Don't worry my child', she mutters in half sleep, caressing my hair

'Hum'

'Even the darkest night will definitely come to an end and the Sun will rise again. Sleep well, don't keep awake', she warns

She knows, am in distress

Granny understands me, reads my heart, absorbs my pains and sorrows like no one else

I shut my eyes, but sleep doesn't come easy

English class test is around the corner, during this weekend. I must give my heart and soul and make it to the top. Grabbing the first spot should be my aim. Mostly, I secure a place from first to third in class tests. In fact, that's the biggest luxury I enjoy among my fellow students in the class. It gives a lot of inflation to my ego

Another consolation is my English teacher Ms. Theresa. She is delicate with me. Maybe because am faring well in her subject. Her son Joyce fares well too. In Joyce,

I find my best friend and sympathizer. There is another secret pact behind. I help him in English tests, but duly ensuring his score doesn't surpass mine. He is aware of my underlying selfishness, but never minds that. In return, he helps me in Physics and Maths. Despite his generosity, I miserably fail to score passing grades in both subjects!

Granny yells something. I stare at her face for a while. She is having a dream, I guess. Can an extremely old person get to see dreams? Who knows! She is in deep sleep. I tightly shut my eyes and embrace her. She is warm, warm like a blanket. Here is the human being who loves me the most! If God permits, she will cross over to the other side of the Earth to see me happy and in peace!

Chapter 4

It's sports time. Sunny hot afternoon. Our school has a vast play area, but is not done up to the level of a modern standardized facility to attract students into sport and games. Dry grey patches everywhere and one could see hardly any grass-covered area. Pits and pebbles mostly. Some boys in my class trying their hands at football. Am not very fond of this game where in, one ball is chased by 20 odd guys!

Physical trainer, who has the looks and size of a Sumo wrestler is imparting practice batch wise. We are Class VI students now, but considered as kiddies. No wonder, we haven't grown up physically either. Trainer is busy explaining tactics on basic dribbling and accurate man-to-man passes. In the process, he steps on the football and loses control. He falls flat on his belly arousing big waves of laughter around him. He has grown heavily sideways with thick adipose collection above hip area on both sides. Looks really funny if you look at the pain it takes when his head-to-toe frame moves around after football!

Girl students generally don't visit the playground unless for Annual sports competitions or Science exhibitions.

This could be the reason why boys' spirit seems dampened, due to the absence of charming spectators in Rising Blue miniskirts and pearl white shirts!

Someone quietly pricks me from behind. I turn back. It's Joyce.

He points towards the long veranda of senior students. Our classes are separated with stairs from higher divisions. Come downstairs, and left side is the playground. Hop down from the playground as there are no stairs or ramp, cross a small area of free clean land rolled with sand, you are right in front of senior division classes.

It's distinctly visible from where we stand. I notice regional language teacher of senior grade is chasing a student. The student is smartly outplaying the teacher and the teacher is trying, frequently swinging the cane in his right hand, but in futile. Every time he gets near to the student within the striking distance, the student skilfully evades the attack jumping and hopping like a seasoned Kabbadi player!

In a flash, now I see the face of the student. It's none other than my elder brother, Nakul bhaiya!

The teacher seems to be Mr. Neelkand, a senior dignified faculty

I turn my face half left. Joyce too is amused. And why wouldn't he be? It's truly hilarious!

Next day, I learn from Joyce that in a regional language class test, Nakul bhaiya draws the picture of a duck leading a raft of ducks with a few ducklings. Though the painting is colourful and attractive, Mr. Neelkand was not so amused. The rest is history!

Joyce gets to know such classified news from his mom, our Class teacher Ms. Theresa. Nakul bhaiya was the subject of discussion in the faculty room the previous day. Some staff find fault with Nakul bhaiya for being a spoiled brat while some other staff criticised the high-handedness of the senior faculty for publicly displaying his might arbitrarily against a budding teenager!

Any school management doesn't spare you for such out of the box offences. Nakul bhaiya is ordered to take Appa to school the next day and meet the Headmistress, Ms. Agnes and Mr. Neelkand to avoid severe disciplinary action.

I come to know from Joyce that Nakul bhaiya would be rusticated if he fails to produce Appa in the school

However, Nakul bhaiya ropes in his closest ally, Amma. After 2 days, another hot and humid afternoon, Amma appears in the school to meet Ms. Agnes. I accompany her to the office as liaison officer as Nakul bhaiya' s entry is temporarily prohibited inside the school compound till an amicable settlement is reached between Appa at one side and Ms. Agnes with Mr. Neelkand at the other.

Now, that Amma is appearing on behalf of Appa as counsellor for Nakul bhaiya, am not quite sure about the end product of this meeting..

Seeing me first at her office entrance, Headmistress signals me to get in. I go inside and present a draft of the situation. Headmistress keeps moving her body in her pompous rolling chair having a posh Red colour upholstery cushioned seat

'Call her in', Ms. Agnes

I come out and get inside a second time with Amma

Seeing both of us together, Ms. Agnes aimlessly makes a full 360-degree rotation in her chair. After a few seconds, the chair comes to a scratchy halt in its previous position. I chuckle seeing that, but with some hard techniques over my nerves, am able to stop my adrenaline rush. Why did she swirl around then? She just displayed her plush office gear, nothing else

Ms. Agnes got transferred from a reputed English medium school controlled by the same diocese. She speaks poor English with lots of formatting errors. Therefore, when she speaks, she ultimately ends up becoming a laughing stock

Ms. Agnes presses the bell. Here appears the peon

'Call Mr. Neelkand'

She again looks at us

After a few minutes, appears Mr. Neelkand, a well-built mid-aged raw person with tough looks and a 2-day old bush beard

Amma explains everything with no much confidence

Ms. Agnes looks at Amma like seeing an Alien from another planet

Ms. Agnes castigates Amma in high-sounding words and phrases in very ordinary English. Poor Amma is caught off guard. Headmistress is in no mood to spare Nakul bhaiya for the atrocity he had created

To Amma's great relief, Headmistress conclusively mutters some sentences in regional language

Thankfully, before coming to school, Amma had a subject session with our neighbour Ms. Miranda in the morning. She lives in our neighbourhood and is our family well-wisher. She is a senior faculty in the English department of our school. Her support remains Amma's only hope

Here, Mr. Neelkand doesn't budge. He argues that the whole episode brought him humiliation and did irreparable damage to his image and repute as a senior staff. Besides, the fact that he ended up at the losing side in the subject track and field event with Nakul bhaiya in the open air, added insult to injury. After all those energy-sapping Zumba dance movements in the veranda, his cane couldn't touch Nakul bhaiya, was probably playing in the back of his mind!

After a solid 15-minute high-octane discussion, floored and without choice, eventually, Amma takes her trump card out. She excuses herself for a minute and brings in Ms. Miranda

Ms. Miranda and Headmistress belong to the same diocese, and needless to say, those from the same diocese share a special bond. If you are a student of a Catholic school or happen to maintain close acquaintance with Christianity, you will understand this better. Ms. Miranda speaks to the Headmistress, and eventually, Ms. Agnes agrees to permit Nakul bhaiya to continue in the school, but on one condition-

'Nakul must win First prizes in Painting and Light Music competitions in the upcoming District Schools Youth Festival. I think the dates are fixed before the final exam'. Ms. Agnes gives her verdict

'If he doesn't win top prizes for the school, he's out', she declares with anguish without the pounding of gavel on the table. She sounds like a judge, truly

Mr. Neelkand, now succumbs to pressure from Ms. Agnes and leaves the office with Ms. Miranda

Amma expresses deep gratitude to Headmistress with folded hands and leaves her office. After descending the stairs, as a customary practice followed by siblings of the same school, I accompany Amma till the exit gate. Seeing Amma, Nakul bhaiya makes a sudden appearance from his hideout just outside the school gate

Amma promptly stuffs a 1-rupee note in his shirt's pocket as though he brought grace and laurels to our family!

Going ahead, Nakul bhaiya's name becomes synonym with several painting competitions at various levels. And he wins accolades for the school in District level arts competitions in the next year too, is another situational irony!

Further, he ultimately earns the unpopular name and fame of becoming a noted dropout from IX grade after successively serving in the same class for 3 years..

And, that is The End of Nakul bhaiya's academic career!

His credentials in District Youth Festivals don't help him to his advantage in the exams. His name and fame adorably limited to the school notice board with print reports and photos of prizes and certificates he won for the school

Whenever I cross this corner, I give a look at those accreditations. It makes my eyes wet..

Scene transition

Friday morning. Perhaps, the most sought after weekday; for this is the last day of the week and what follows are Saturday and Sunday, 2 consecutive holidays. Anyone gets into a class room on a Friday morning will easily catch the mood of students. It's entertainingly noisy. The surrounding noise gives a high for the students!

Right after the morning assembly session, all are involved in keen discussions about the weekend program. Pupils who live in nearby locations to each other choke out a plan to meet for meals or play matches. Some so-called intellects even plan for a weekend combined study

May please note, our teachers and Headmistress have high opinion about us. And why not, given that magical aura surrounding us of the tag of 'Brilliant Students', though blown out of real proportions, they can legitimately expect excellent results. Their analysis is justifiable at least on paper, from their point of view!

But today morning, am thrilled about something. English class test is to begin in a few minutes from now. Here's where I must settle scores with all Maths lovers. So far, my marks have been close to maximum, which is far ahead of what class toppers score in Maths. Here is my Golden chance straight from the Heaven, extended by The Almighty God, only for me

Enters Ms. Theresa, my favourite among all teaching staff. Being the Class teacher, she records attendance in the morning. She makes a note of regular absentees, English Haters, in other words, Patriots of regional language!

She has the looks and mannerisms of a no-nonsense college dean. By virtue of being the English teacher, she shows off a dose of extra grandiose here and there. She exactly knows when and where to apply her weight. Leave it apart, she teaches her subject exquisitely well, digging out the deepest roots of the language. She gives herself entirely and absolutely into every minute detail of the grammar and prose. Her dedication is of the highest order. Even the dullest of the students sitting in the farthest corner will sharpen their ears showing interest. Her depth of skill and assiduity, I can never come across in any teacher anywhere! When it comes to ethics of this noble profession, she simply ticks almost all the boxes!

Attendance process is over. She slowly comes around and distributes question papers, and finishes it in 5 minutes

'Has everyone gotten the question paper in your hand, huh? It's her style of preparation before asking students to start writing

'Yes teacher', our single voice

'Kay, take your answer sheets. Be cool and calm. Don't be generous to your neighbour and don't copy from the idiot sitting next to you. He will write some rubbish and you are most likely to copy the same taking it as the perfect answer you are desperately looking for', Ms. Theresa

'Pen in your hand now', her next instruction

Ms. Theresa looks around to catch any possible defaulter who's not yet ready

'Good'. She convinces herself

'Start now', her Command. She sounds like the gunshot given to the sprinters who are ready on starting blocks. She is technically thorough in this arena. No loopholes to students

It looks like, everyone is hurrying up to start with as though the chance is given on a 'first come, first serve basis', and if they get late to make it to the front, there wouldn't be any further chance!

Some fellows I can find, looking at the question paper and Ms. Theresa alternatively, pretending to be in the know of all answers

However, the anxious 40 minutes are over

She is collecting answer sheets from the students. I could notice some mediocre students make last-minute dig as if to pen down a full page!

It looks as if they can reproduce all correct answers in another 2 minutes if given an opportunity. But now way

'Hey All, time is up', comes stop memo from Ms. Theresa

She quickly collects answer sheets one by one, organizes it, and keeps it on her table per attendance register serial number

My name loiters somewhere at the last in the attendance register

Other remaining subjects for the days are General Science, Regional language, Social Studies, and Maths the Giant Killer!

I could somehow navigate through the Maths class today without being hurt. It was one of those rare occasions!

Scene transition

On our way back home, Oh, I missed out to mention a crucial element. One of the prime characters-

Her name is Vibha

The most significant person in my boyhood life after Granny. She is Appu uncle's daughter. Appu uncle is Appa's very close friend. They're 3siblings. She's the middle one. Has an older sister, Raji, and younger brother, Bharath

Her physical description: Small in size, egg shaped - slightly oval, but primarily round! A miniature-size cute girl with round face and fair complexion with small little fingers and toes. She wears a 4-inch footwear. I taunt her with funny names synonymous with her pocket-size figure. She looks bubbly and walks like a rolling Rugby ball. She literally crawls with her small little feet along the road moving at a tortoise' pace. If there is a slow-walk competition, she would easily grab the first spot!

Her house has a frontage main road, a better one than ours. Whereas, my house is located about 200mtrs down somewhere in the middle of our housing colony. In the mornings, I would reach her house and we make it to school together on foot. We talk anything under the sun except Maths. We both are in the same grade. She being a regional language student, I usually tease her about her lack of knowledge in English. She rarely fights or argues with me. Simply smiles, and sometimes pinches me on my sleeves. We would walk 2kms and reach school, and in the evenings, same exercise in reverse

Our friendship is purely innocent and based on no terms or conditions. Our togetherness generates enormous joy and fun!

We walk back home. Slow leisurely steps. I rearrange my steps time and again to be in alignment with her slow speed. I throw small stones at the kittens and puppies and oddly seen cocks and hens on the wayside

'Don't do that Sanju', Vibha forbids me holding my hand

'Why're you giving pain to these poor creatures, are you happy seeing them in pains, huh'?

She is annoyed seeing me do cruel things to fellow creatures who can't express their agony like humans

'It's just fun Vibha, I don't mean to cause any pain to them', my casual reply

'You get daily lashes at your Amma's hands and still don't improve yourself. You are like a dog's tail, never straightens. It's fun for you, but pain for them', Vibha is furious and Philosophic

She is not in a mood to spare me that soon

'Okay, crawl faster you Lilliputian', I mock

'What's that you've called me'? 'You flag post', she shoots back, taking a jibe at my lean frame

'You are a Lilliputian. Name of the islander in Jonathan Swift's Gulliver's Travels where the folks are hardly 6 inches tall, but pretend to be more than a full-sized human. You're acting too much, like them', I share my general knowledge in literature without mincing words

'One day, I will pull your tongue out and clip it with staplers'; I warn her losing my cool

'I'll not accompany you to school tomorrow', Vibha

'Don't care a damn', my retaliation

'You don't realize the suffering of other creatures. You are cruel to me, cruel to animals as well. Not for nothing that you get lashed from your mother. It's futile to argue with you..', Vibha

'Enough. Please stop it', I said

'Trying to correct your mistakes is like helping a baby elephant to don a pair of trunks. Unthinkable and sheer waste of time. And the whole process ends up becoming an amusement to the onlooker'! Vibha goes on and on..

'So, you're happy that am thrashed by my Amma. No affinity for me. You're no exception', my words suddenly fumble in pain

Short silence

'You are also like my mother. She finds pleasure like a sadist in thrashing me. She has no remorse seeing me fall down and writhe in pain. And you are supporting such a cruel mother. Don't speak to me henceforth', I briskly walk ensuring that she is not catching up with my pace

She doesn't open her mouth till we reach home

We reach her house and I don't wave my fingers and say Bye, which I normally do

She gives a gloomy look at me and goes inside. I couldn't read her face

My feet pick up speed way down to my house

Its 10 minutes past 5 when I stepped inside my house

I immediately slip into my domestic clothes, take pots and run to the corporation tap. It's my pretention, for somehow, I need to please Amma to escape from her cane for being late. I can't disclose that I brought Vibha along back from school. Amma is not very fond of Vibha for reasons unknown. Amma in fact, doesn't like me keep good company with any girl in my locality

My life's caged. No free interaction with friends. Kite flying restricted to one single day, only on the big festival day. Strict timings to school and back. And be her domestic help and follow her orders religiously. Without slightest of a deviation

All my friends learned swimming, but I didn't. She didn't allow me visit the nearby ponds. Am unhappy of having a pale and spiritless boyhood. No excitement

Going ahead, what will I cherish in my memories?

I have a deep sigh

Our municipal corporation tap provides non-stop water supply. Clear tasty water without odour. I fill the pots and fetch them back home. Besides, fill the big storing pots and then return back to the tap. Make 4 or 5 trips

'Enough', Amma puts a sudden brake to my free water delivery service. 'Now, drink coffee and go to studies. I'll go to market and come'

Her instructions are beyond any Appeal, like Supreme Court division bench order

Another hectic day is coming to close. It's 7, and Amma is back from market. She straightaway hits the kitchen

Chapter 5

Granny is silent. She doesn't do much of a talking today. It's not usual. Granny goes into silent mode only in rarest of rare cases. Mostly, the reason would be quarrel with Amma and in the middle, might be Amma used some insubordinate language. Let it be, to me, silence is Golden now. I shouldn't poke my silly nose into the centre of their personal affairs

I open my text book. Can't find the right frame of mind to concentrate

Somi is helping Amma in the kitchen. This is unusual. It scarcely happens. Probably, Somi wants to please Amma for some gains. She bribes Amma through pleasing techniques

I fake some reading. A favourite lesson from English Text, The Merchant of Venice

Mind slips off. What has hit me today?

Maybe, my fight with Vibha is causing hindrance. Perhaps, my behaviour was unscrupulous. I hurt her. Might be, she is right. I must learn to feel the sufferings of other beings. But then, she did hurt me too. She spoke a little too far. Supported my cruel mother, which really kills me..

Am going to remain cross with her, but how long? Vibha is very special to me, and how can I remain aloof or keep myself emotionally distant from her? I don't think this squabble with Vibha is going to survive beyond tonight. It stabs me with a dagger from within when I come to think of walking away from someone who am in passionate friendship with! It's a pity that am incapacitated to vent out my feelings more amiably. Let me test the waters tomorrow. I must end this dilemma of emotional conflicts straight tomorrow, and not beyond!

I've my supper as fast as I could, as though there is no tomorrow and it's my proverbial Last Supper

I feel like going to bed soon. Granny is in a drowsy mood. It looks like; she is not interested to connect with me at the moment

Lying down flat on bare mattress and cover the head with thick cotton sheets. And unleash your thoughts. Leave the reins loose and the result is a magical confluence of enormously beautiful events and characters come on to the stage one after another, which you would never accomplish in real life. It's a truly fascinating mind exercise. It takes you across deep sea..lush green forest.. misty mountains..serene islands..a host of beautifully dancing Peruvian lilies and so on..

Am happy with my wild imaginations. It keeps me cool. It gives me immense relief. One's own thoughts are the real sources of action in life, and the very same thoughts give birth to fascinating by-products, which change your moods from the roots!

I uncork my mind and soul and let it fly like a bird out of the cage to glide around. After a short while, I gently sink into infinity and embrace sleep like a lullaby induces an infant to sleep in the cradle! A mother's sweet lullabies work wonders to foster a strong bond with her and the child, so is the case with me and my wandering soul as well in the world of Animation!

Outside, heavy wind blows across. A sudden heavy downpour lashes across. I can hear rain pattering on the roof top. It's rhythmic. Music to my ears, it has always been!

'Sanju..Sanju, its past 8.30, get up child', it's Granny's voice, piercing my eardrums

I spring up from the mattress and make Sukhasana position as though am going to be served with a grand-gala morning feast

'Do you know Sanju; there was heavy thunder shower with heavy windstorm howling the whole night. I was very much scared. Uma Aunt's half of the roof flown away. Nattu chacha's bicycle was washed away to Udhay's backyard'

'Your Amma's fancy sari is found lying in mud', she giggles. Granny generously showcases her pleasure

It's close to 9. Am hurrying up to school, 'won't speak to Vibha', I assure myself

'Hey Sanju, Vibha left long ago. Where were you, huh? Run and catch up with her', Vibha's elder sister Raji shouts from behind

I don't care a heck. There's still light drizzle. My legs are picking up pace

Scene transition

Our Science teacher is a middle-aged, stout, typically traditional man. Bald with a big tummy and he wears a frightened look on his face. Has a big bulgy pair of eyes having lifeless rubberized eyeballs, it looks like. He has shiny chubby cheeks like that of an infant. Reddish complexion. His name is Mr. Gagan

Joyce says, he is the son of an Army man and was born in North India. Now I get to know, how he speaks with a North Indian accent

It's the Second period in the afternoon, maybe past 3 or so. Mr. Gagan narrates about Ferdinand Magellan, the popular Portuguese explorer who undertakes the historical voyage, the very first expedition to circumnavigate the world. Thus, proving to the world that the Earth is spherical in shape. He is going ga-ga over it somewhere in the middle..

Mr. Gagan's expressions are heavy and gives pressure to words wherever it's not very appropriate. He strains a lot while speaking English, especially, while explaining some special episodes from History, like the one, on in the class. He probably tries to enact the character and toils up to the hilt to bring out the true events right in front of the class a touch of creative beauty!

Almost half time down the line, he now looks like a boxer who is just out of the ring having finished 10 rounds of action with a far superior challenger. His cheeks are now more reddish, and sweat drops rolling down. We can see narrow canals of sweat on his forehead and flowing through his face, neck, and dripping further down. He is so tired in action that he looks down and out. I can even see a big drop of sweat fall on the lecture table and breaks

Mr. Gagan eventually throws his heavy body into the chair as though he doesn't want the chair next day. It makes a creaky noise unable to bear his disproportionate weight. However, the chair adjusts itself and fully contains his overflowing physique

Teacher's seat is like a barber's chair, that fits all buttocks!

Mr. Gagan's boxing session is over in another 15 minutes. The last 15 minutes, he has been inactive. He seems to have given up the fight!

'Trinnnng', the short bell rings to notify the period is over. Mr. Gagan gets up from the seat with noticeable effort and walks out. His gaits are not in alignment with his body

Faculty is not available during the last 2 sessions. Class makes hell of a noise when the faculty gets late to report

First free period passes without any mishap. No standby. It's now the second free period, the last part of the day. Am counting every minute to jump out from the frying pan!

Headmistress, Ms. Agnes usually takes stroll inside the school compound. She randomly makes her entry into classes where the faculty is absent. She has a Jet Black complexion with an overall unpleasant body language. Well built with Black tiny eyes like that of an elephant. She stammers quite a bit and still tries speaking with pace as though answering rapid fire questions in a quiz competition

Students find her very much excited while she converse in English with other graded staff. She poses herself as a very strict Administrator, but everyone knows that she got a punishment transfer to our school for being casually lousy and poor in administration and bringing disgrace to her previous school.

However, she is of the view that she is surrounded by a plethora of knowledge and wisdom!

She peeps inside our class like the bride-to-be curiously peeping through the tiny door cavity at the handsome young man who is anxiously awaiting her entry into the hall with a tray of sweets and beverages!

We spot those small eyes and identify her easily. She makes an unwelcome entry with her heavy feet. Then, there is a pin-drop silence in the Class. No, we are not scared with the presence of Headmistress or the cane loosely hanging in her left arm, but as a matter of fact, we are terribly concerned that what if Ms. Agnes takes over as lecturer for the period as a stopgap! Well, in that case, given her known credentials, the session could a glorious disaster!

We had horrifying experience in the past. The fate of being in her class means, the state of Jonathan trapped in the fort of Dracula. You can't escape unless Dracula goes out leaving you unshackled!

The whole Class is frozen for moment foreseeing the immediate stroke of ill luck. Ms. Agnes notices that the class is calm and well disciplined, she retrieves

'Trinnnnng', here goes the long bell. Another boxing day is over

Coming out of the class, I go to Regional language division looking for Vibha. Poor girl. I didn't even care to give a smile while parting yesterday. I behaved awkward having not taken her along today morning. I feel embarrassed. She is not seen there

Somewhat disturbed, I take the stairs down to the field. 'What if she doesn't care to look at me'..

Can't find her anywhere in the field. I go to the girls' washroom area and wait outside for a while

Want to check with some of her peers I know

'She left early today', the bespectacled classmate of Vibha informs. She looks plump and owns a husky voice. She has stubborn expressions perfectly in line with her rough looks

Way back home, I've pains in my chest

Feet are not moving. Am upset. Asking myself too many disturbing questions

'Why did she leave early?

'Why didn't she tell me before leaving the school'?

'What if she doesn't speak to me tomorrow morning'?

Several questions pop up

Too many Ifs and Buts. Mind is disorganized. Lose my peace again

Without doubt, Vibha is another human being after my Granny who I believe to be closest to me. She helps me in simple ways and tricks whenever am in soup

I've developed emotional dependency on both

She creates a clean and tidy poster out of me in our neighbourhood

Losing her means, nothing but I cease to exist

'What if she doesn't speak to me ever again'? Can't really think of it

Overall, am the most desirable among boys in my neighbourhood. They pamper me for being good student. They demand my services to write letters in English for someone living faraway or read a wire and translate, fill up a check leaf, or get passbooks updated from the bank, or accompany them to the manager if the clerk shows reluctance in giving proper service e.t.c., e.t.c., I see some of the bank staff generally act too big to their grades. And I think a few of them possess a super-inflated ego just for no big reason. Yes, may be because they safeguard the nation's wealth in cash!

People around in my locality hold me in high regard as am a handy tool for all, technically though

Surprisingly, the odd factor is, am not so dearly wanted in my home except for my Granny and Appa, whereas, am 'The Most Wanted'everywhere else!

Night. Pitch dark inside my small room with the Kerosene lamp turned off long ago

Night wears off little by little. I struggle to overcome a sleepless night once again

Morning. No freshness of spirit. Today is another public holiday. No school. It means, can't get to see Vibha. Uninspiring long hours to pass before I can have a glimpse of her again

The day I can't see Vibha, is dry and dull

I curse all public holidays. I must see her tomorrow and conciliate her

No choice. I resign to the fate of affairs as of now!

Chapter 6

Today, I've some scores to settle with Ramesh. He has been getting the better of me in this game since a great deal of time. Recent memories of debacles I had at his hands hover around in my mind while I run to the playground. Long ago, this land was a paddy field, but no cultivation ever since I can remember. It has become a vast dry land over the years. Boys from the neighbourhood community converted into a play area over a span of years

This field has all the features of a waste land. It's now an open multipurpose park, of course, without any modern amenities. Adults and elderly come here to take leisurely walk. During festival seasons, one can see giant circus tents erected here or meal topped with village games and music and sometimes, exhibitions of vintage stamps and coins or a cultural show or a traditional stage drama. In addition, during New Year or Christmas, short film shows are conducted by the local NGO body. But, no charming or flattering colour films. No glamorous hero or heroine. No song and dance. Some old Black & White grey movies based on pre-independence era. Or maybe, the theme would be India's struggle for Independence, Bengal famine, or tragic aftermaths of Indo-Pak partition and so on. Totally dry stuff which can't incite curiosity in our minds. In my memory, the best movie I've seen here is a Hollywood blockbuster, Ben-Hur

Am feeling a new-found vigour today. It's born out of my thirst to win over Ramesh. It charges me up. Am fully synergized from my toes. I must push him today to the wall and beyond before I hit the sack tonight

In the field, there's our gang eagerly waiting for Ramesh and me

'Hello', I wave at them, Rajesh's not seen in the near vicinity

'Come Sanju. Are you ready'? Friends shout

Their clamouring stirs up a strong feel of zeal within me. Sparks originate and crisscross violently inside my brain, and I can sense the energy pump into my extremities

I look at me. Goosebumps? Not at all. Am still within the limits of my nerves

Here is Ramesh. He is fresh from the nearby water pool. There are rectangle shaped water pools around. These are our Desi swimming pools. All my friends are good swimmers at this age other than me. Am the odd figure out throughout. Deprived of many glitters of a childhood!

Ramesh is a very good swimmer. He bravely dives into the deep pool and plucks water lilies and seeds of the beautiful Pink-hued Lotus from the mud filled bottom. He is daring and proactive. He dives and swims around, makes many laps to and fro very fast like a professional freestyle swimmer!

Except that am studying in a reputed school and tall and fair complexioned; by the way, fairness, I naturally inherited from Amma, I've no merit or virtue that puts me ahead of my friends. I carry some inherent apprehensions too, which force me to genuinely doubt about the prospects of my big future

Time is running out. May be, half past 5 or beyond

Sun is fast sinking at the West. Setting Sun is enchantingly beautiful. There is a strong promise of the universe in every sunset. The promise of a new dawn. The promise of a new sunrise, and along with that comes new hope..new life. In that respect, very sunset is a mark of new beginnings!

I simply love that glorious scene at the horizon. I wonder, when people mostly like sunrise than sunset, what's that which makes me fall for sunset?

Between the Sun and human lives on Earth, there are certain curious questions, and you can't really find an answer!

I look at Ramesh. He and his sister have a peculiar colour complexion. A mix of Red and Brown. Amma once says it's congenital, occurred due to some severe deficiency of a particular vitamin ingredient when they're carried in the womb. He is tall and has a flat body. Sun rays fall on his skin and make colourful strides of reflection

Honestly, am envy of his certain abilities. Firstly, he is a good swimmer. Equipped with better acumen. During our games, when a crunch situation arises, he reads the game well and traps me. He anticipates the game very well and foresees my next move. Before I read his trick, the game is over. He wins in style with his trademark lip-corner smile. A clever guy!

It's too late. Probably close to 6. I once again look at the West horizon. The Sun has almost sunk in the Arabian Sea. The sky now looks like a brilliantly made canvas by a genius painter who made a cocktail of Red and Orange colours and splashed on to it!

It looks simply spectacular. Beyond words. Can't turn my eyes away. Whenever I get to see such a sunset, my heart absorbs the scene withal its beauty and charm without a drop being dropped!

Perfectly matching with the beautiful sunset, a full moon in the making tonight

I slowly walk into the middle

'So..no action today? Ramesh's ready. Give your best shot, only 10 minutes. You must turn it around today. He's acting too much Sanju'. Atchu's voice filled with passion having added a trace of revenge

Atchu's my next door guy, Uma aunt's son. Third among siblings, younger to Baby. They're 5 siblings. He is the coolest guy among all my friends. His IQ level is slightly below average. Skipped studies even before it was begun, I suppose

'No, Atchu, time's up. Amma's alert call will come any time soon', I say

Not waiting for their response, I take a brisk walk back home. I know, no friends would follow me. They enjoy the happiness of freedom and togetherness. Am certain, one day, they'll make better, independent, and confident citizens than me. What's so great in having a mere 'Good Boy' tag and score marks in selective subjects when you can't spread your wings and fly around and discover yourself! Their parents may be inferior to mine in certain ways and means, but they're more accommodative and easy going. Above all, they trust their children!

In fact, no progress card has genuinely assessed the raw talent and competency of any child ever. It's not possible!

'Come fast Sanju; are you so tired or what'? Somi's arrogance

'Don't shout, Amma will hear', I said

'Amma is annoyed. Nakul bhaiya is hungry and is throwing tantrums all over. I've seasonal Asthmatic issues, you know that, can' do any work', Somi

'When're you doing any, huh? I wash your uniform even when you are keeping well and free of attacks. You are thankless. You've this habit of poking to Amma all nonsensical things about me, 'am furious

No response from Somi

'Sanju, go to the teashop and get some vadai and milk tea, and come fast', comes Amma to the scene as though she is suddenly air dropped

She hands to me a 2 rupee note and a Hammer Master Hansa flask to fetch hot milk tea

Nearest teashop consumes a good 25-minute walk up and down. My rubber slippers stopped giving services close to 1 month ago. That poor thing has given away its maximum life and beyond till date. I run on barefoot. Must make it fast, or else, I might be seeing Nakul bhaiya's anguish as well. Face to face encounter with Nakul bhaiya could end up disastrous tome. His age could be somewhere between 15 and 16, but he acts more than Appa. I normally avoid a faceoff with him. I don't have the bravery to stand straight in front of him. Few of his friends are generally older to him and he too acts the same. Granny knows that he is slipping into wrongful acquaintances, but it's not easy to convince Amma to set him right. He skips being at home the major part of the day. We don't get to see Nakul bhaiya at home after school hours or on Sundays and holidays

'Nakul is flying too high Sulo; that which goes up has to come down one day, beware. Try bringing him back to track' Granny frequently warns Amma

Amma doesn't heed to Granny's words, but is quite perturbed about every single minute movement of mine. She has a questionnaire kept ready for me. What I do? Where I go? Who are my friends..interrogation.. intriguing cross-examinations at the slightest breach of her commands!

My boyhood is going through emotional strangulation. No buyers for my lament. Live like orphaned!

On way back, am engulfed in weird thoughts. No one understands my small little pains and aches other than my Granny. Even if I commit the most heinous crime, Granny wouldn't take a second to coddle me in her lap and fight the whole world. That's the depth of her love. There's no second thought. Sadly, she is seldom heard. Not even Appa lend her his ears since long. He is a simple cool person gotten lost in the hurly-burly of daily life. Still struggles to figure out the nuances of his own family. Constantly wrestles with life to turn a new leaf every day!

I've great respect and love for my Appa. He pays special care to my studies, books, other amenities. But, some of my essentialities are not in his control. Nakul bhaiya and Somi get almost everything they ask for, but are the last child and my exigencies too are the last priority. My place is always at the back burner. Nakul bhaiya is Amma's all-season favourite and Somi makes a close second

I remain neglected and maligned everywhere like Karna of Mahabharat. The ancient epic is my all time favourite. It contains legendary characters, like Arjun, Eklavya, Abhimanu, Kunti, Draupadi...and the list doesn't end here. The portrayal of each character by Granny during her story session makes them even more illustrious and extraordinary. I tend to think more specifically of Karna. There are many gut-wrenching occasions in Mahabharat when Karna's very own individuality and integrity were abused right under the nose of his famed near and dear ones. He was generous. His battle skill was nonpareil. But still, Karna - the great warrior was belittled everywhere right from the beginning till the end of the great epic!

Where I stand? I want an answer

'Am home', I shout from the door

Amma storms out and snatches the polythene parcel and disappears inside in a single stroke. She acts as though am the root cause of all her distress

Amma's association with me is imbalanced. Unscrupulous. And her attitude is never going to change

I sit in the cordoned veranda at the back yard. It's partially damaged. Our house constructively looks big with old fashioned thatched roof made of dried palm leave sat the rear side with partially tiled roof in the facade. Overall, it doesn't give a pleasing look to the eyes. Severely lacks maintenance due to scarcity of funds. Wooden doors with loose hinges are in dilapidated condition. I lie down flat staring through the roof. Harsh weather takes its toll on the ceiling. There are uncountable hollow pockets. My eyes penetrate through the holes and reach the sky. Lying down flat on my stomach, I count the stars. Roof has long ago exceeded its lifespan and screaming for some urgent repair loud and clear!

I hear indistinct noise from the kitchen. Utensils make some clack sound. Some diminished traces of conversation of Amma and Somi. I often find Somi speaks into Amma's ears as if she is selling the country's Nuclear secrets to undesirables!

It's too late, but need a bathe before I go to sleep. I fill water in the bath and take a superfast bathe like a crow

Back, I insert my legs inside a pair of old Khaki trunks, which are no more in use as school uniform. It's Amma's policy directive that I domestically use old uniform Khaki trunks when they're past their expiry dates

'You look cool in that', Somi usually taunts. 'Always in uniform like a soldier showing operational readiness at the borders' and she would giggle

I take it light-heartedly, as a compliment. Do I really have any choice?!

Chapter 7

Granny is shivering like a Malaria patient. It's past midnight. Pinching cold

'What Granny', I suddenly wake up rubbing my eyes. I feel her body warmer than usual

'Don't know my child, am not feeling well after that fall in the toilet. One week ago, she fell flat in the bathroom losing her balance. She is too aged and fragile, and it's high time she had an assistant to take care of her primary health care and fetching for her nature's calls and giving her bath or help change her clothes. But hiring Home Nurse service for Granny is beyond budget for Appa. Granny is well-aware of that. Whatsoever, Amma or Somi ensures that Granny gets regular bath and draped in fresh clothes without missing a day

I rub her palms and feet. Cover her delicate body with blanket

'Shall I get some warm water', am about to cry

Want to awaken Somi sleeping nearby. She is in deep sleep. Her snore resembles that of a Reed instrument used by the Tribes of Venezuelan forest. I was amused to come across this bit of news about this particular tribe recently.

The sound waves end in infinity and then catches up again with regular intervals. Honestly, her snore is not much disturbing

'Not really. You sleep and don't worry about me. I'll be kay in the morning', Granny

'Shall I wake her up?' I point to Somi

'Not at all', Granny

I hug her and close my eyes tight

'I think, my time is nearing', she whispers. Her quavering voice, as if coming from a distant planet horrifies me. My heart trembles. Shaking life a ripen leaf

'Where're you going Granny'? I ask trying hard to control my tears

'Don't know my child. But there is always a time for departure even if there is no place to go. It's for everyone. And you know, I am too old and I can't stretch myself any further'

'I'm worried about you my little heart', Granny grasps my left hand

I know, she is breathing only for my sake..to see me happy..to bring smile on my face!

What if she dies one day, like my younger sister? Of course, with her, I didn't have any sibling-like intimacy, since she departed too early and I don't even remember her face quite well

There can be no one ever to fill Granny's place. There would never be anyone to replace Granny. Such is the impactful presence she makes in my life all along!

My little heart prays to God Narsimhamurthi, the idol of our famous temple, which is very nearby. Some fond memories of the petty teashop near the temple flash in my mind

Friends and me would visit this temple sometimes. We give prior notice to our neighbourhood about our near-future visit to the temple, and accept small coins as offerings. Folks think, by giving offerings to temple, their struggles would be nullified and the God would gift them with a noble life

But poor folks don't have the slightest hint that we collect the offerings, and end up swallowing hot Dosa and coffee from the teashop by exchanging a major chunk of these offerings!

I still have the same taste at the tip of my tongue. When we cross this teashop and approach the temple premises, we strongly feel the aroma of hot steamy Dosa and Red chilli mix coconut chutney, and hot filter coffee wafting out of its kitchen. The feel is unexplainable!

Scene transition

It's a Monday morning. I always hate Monday mornings for unsure reasons. What makes me happy today is, Granny gets up as usual and sips her regular Black filter coffee

I look at her. She gives her trademark Vintage smile. The cutest smile I've ever seen. Her mouth opens to the fullest vertically upward. It's the generous display of her unfeigned delight!

Her open mouth looks like a female vanity bag unzipped. Mysterious interior. Hell with it. I've other significant things today morning!

Finish my morning rituals too early today. Donned my washed and ironed uniform. It has undergone a starch wash. Looks very stiff even without my toothpick-like frame pushed inside. It can even firmly stand independently vertically on the floor!

I carefully comb my hair. Spend those extra few minutes in front of the looking mirror. Apply more Exotica talcum powder on my cheeks and neck. Now, okay. I give 5/5 for my makeup. It's only 8 in the morning, but am already at the doorstep of Vibha. I must sort out the differences in the morning itself when we walk down to school

Seeing me, she comes to the front room and stretches her neck outside like a crane looking for fish in the pond. Her house is well maintained than ours. Her mother's hospitality is awesome. Whenever I visit, her mother, Lakshmi aunt gives me something to eat and a Black filter coffee or sometimes, coffee made in goat milk. Her hospitality is a fine display of love and affection. If there is an exchange offer for my Amma from God, my first choice would be Vibha's mother, Lakshmi aunt!

She gives me pocket money occasionally; especially, when I badly require some coins to buy a notebook or get a roll of thread to fly kites!

If ever I've to return her all these obligations any time in life when I grow up, my several months salary put together wouldn't be enough for a decent payback. There is no substitute for selfless love and innocent bondage of human hearts. It's like a beautiful rainbow. You can't really touch it or quantify it but you can see it when expressed.. feel it with your heart!

If love is not expressed, what's the point of stocking that deep emotion? It becomes a burden. And one day, that unused and unshared love becomes a scrap..no takers, no more in demand!

Vibha is ready. I literally pull her out of the house. She looks at me. Her lips makes a beautiful curve. It's truly wonderful. A smile is a curve that makes many things straight. She has small little dimples too. Looks very cute!

'Where were you that day evening? Why did you pack up early, didn't inform me'? I question her like a policeman

'I wasn't well, so, could not inform you', she answers. 'Then, yesterday was holiday, we couldn't meet'. She adds up, trying to cool me down

She too can't be cross with me for long, I guess

'What's your lunch today in the pack'?, I ask

'Steamed Brown rice with fish fry and dhal smash', Vibha

'Wow! My mouth is drooling

Lakshmi aunt cooks well at par with Amma. I can never forget the taste of her food. I had it several times

'How about you Sanju'

'Nothing for lunch', my casual answer

'Why'? She is eager

'No reason. 'I was in a hurry today morning and didn't wait for food to get ready. No one asked me to wait either'

She just gives a look. As usual, unable to read it

'Heard, you had an English class test recently. Will get the result today'? Vibha

'Hope so. By the way, today's first session is English, I said'. Ms. Theresa might have corrected the answer sheets yesterday. It was a holiday, right'? I get pump up

'Will you make it first'? Vibha knows am good at the tongue

'Not sure, may or may not'

It was 5 past 9 when we entered the school campus

Students lavishly roam around in the open space. All in uniform, but I spot a few defaulters

Suddenly, I think of Nakul bhaiya

The day Amma had come to school to meet our Headmistress, Ms. Agnes, same evening, and Granny locks horns with Amma

'You pamper him a lot. You spoiled him', Granny angrily points at Amma

'None of your deal, don't interfere', Amma warns

'Sulo, 1 stitch in time saves 9, remember that. Don't dance to his tunes', Granny also uses the pruned version of Amma's full name, Sulochana

Amma angrily goes inside and slashes the door. Granny feels hugely insulted!

'Hey, where're you lost'? Vibha pulls my hand and stops me

I go past my class, lost in thoughts. She understands that

'Kay, bye, see you in the evening' I wave my fingers in a peculiar manner as usual

Vibha chuckles and walks away to the girls' division in the first floor

A solid single bell goes in the air

After a short while, Ms. Theresa enters the class. We notice, she has the bunch of answer sheets folded and held in her left hand

Attendance over..and she now, unfolds the bunch of answer sheets

'Sanjay', she calls out my name first; roll number wise, my name comes somewhere at the bottom of the attendance register

'Your score is not up to my expectations', she remarks without announcing my score

That's her style. She never announces the marks scored by the student

She went on to call all names roll number wise. Picks some back benchers and a few front benchers as well, that includes me

She gives me a slight dressing. She is not very impressed with my score. I read from her face

I make a poor Third! Might be, I was overconfident or rather I've undermined the top Two scorers; one, a distant friend, son of another teaching staff of our school, and the other one, Rose, the same cool bubbly girl with sleepy eyes. She normally lies low. No one in the class ever expected her to be the dark Horse. And ya, she has a mystery smile on her lips while receiving the answer sheet. Truly indefinable smile. It will take a Herculean task to decode her smile!

Another dream shatters into tiny pieces. My heart is aching. Just couldn't make it. Even the smallest of my wishes is not fulfilled. No destined to come true!

May be, Almighty God doesn't want to see me a winner. Precisely, Lord Narsimhamurthi didn't bless me, for I misappropriate the offerings meant for him given by the believers. As full offerings do not reach his Hundi, barring some tits and bits, Narsimhamurthi is punishing me!

Am utterly silent in the evening on way back home. I feel like crying

Vibha reads my mind well. She is also silent

Chapter 8

Final exams got over. Summer vacation just got over

Am seamlessly promoted to Standard VII, of course, Vibha too!

Nakul bhaiya picks me for almost everything and he connects it with my attitude. He feels am not seriously prepared enough to be in Class VII. Of late, he doesn't miss any opportunity to pick me. He pokes to Amma against me; this was not his habit earlier. And a trivial accusation against me, baseless or worth a hearing, Amma doesn't miss a minute to spank me if her cane has not come handy quickly anywhere around. Her cane is the cruellest weapon my childhood has ever seen!

On a Sunday, Nakul bhaiya happens to see me play with my friend Suresh and his brother Sunil

'Leave them and go to studies, your portions are tough', Nakul bhaiya

'It's 12 noon, I will get to studies after lunch. And the school has just opened', I politely say

Nakul bhaiya loses his cool. Cuts down 2thick stalks from my pet Mulberry tree, braids it together and rushes to me. Seeing Nakul bhaiya coming at me hammer and tongs, Suresh and Sunil vaporize in the atmosphere. Being physically weak, am the proverbial lamb to the slaughter. I can foresee what'd he up to. Am too meek to resist. I become small little cat drenched in the rain!

I frantically look for shelter. Run towards Granny who is busy chewing betel leaf. Granny can't do much to stop Nakul bhaiya by any means

Having left school, he has gotten a lot of free time to mooch around. He has recently joined Kalaripayattu and proudly toning up his body. He is athletic and strong. He is a fast runner. Fetched prizes at the district level school games and festival competitions. This apart, he is good at light music and drawing. Amalgamation of all these qualities and talents in right proportions, no doubt, he carries that X-factor in him!

Blessed with all these virtues though, he possesses a big negative. Indiscipline. Doesn't care a damn about good values of life. Nothing bothers him too much. Laid-back kind of a guy

He is highly influential in the family. Appa normally avoids a direct confrontation with him, for Amma never allows Appa to advise or correct him for offences not expected of his age. I could often feel a faint redolence of cigarette smoke hung on his clothes. Nakul bhaiya has become the biggest 'what if' in our family!

'Then you deal with him Sulo', Appa resigns. He is accustomed to meek submissions under pressure from situational compulsions. Leaves him to Amma to take over the scene

In Amma, Nakul bhaiya finds his strongest backer and mentor. Amma stands tall against all odds to protect him

'He provided me the fortune of motherhood', Amma boasts frequently during family assemblies amidst any mix-up involving Nakul bhaiya!

I run and get beneath a wooden couch. It's an old obsolete piece of furniture. It's main frame gave away when 2 months ago, Amma's maternal uncle paid us a visit and planned to rest his back after a hearty mid-day meal served. He is a customarily a fat man with a waist size anywhere between 44 and 48 inches. The seat gave up unable to contain his weight. In the process, the top frame of the couch broke and caved in taking the shape of a trapezium. One more thing, its legs are missing too since then. Somi says, Amma used it as firewood one day

Thank God, Amma's uncle didn't fracture his spine

Amma ensures good hospitality whenever her relatives visit us. On such occasions, Amma cooks rich food, fish and mutton delicacies with coconut milk-banana smoothie as wash down. But such occasion infrequent - few and far between. Amma cooks the tastiest food. No one in the entire locality can match her cooking skills. A mastery of hers, worth mention though!

Oops! Nakul bhaiya looks very very impulsive..in a belligerent mood..

He pulls me out and slashes me mercilessly with the Mulberry strands. After a few minutes he leaves me crawling. Discharge from eyes, nose, and mouth, I make a very pathetic poster of myself indeed!

Amma comes from outside with Somi. They're on a flying visit to the neighbourhood. Amma gives a passing glance at me, no, she barely has seen me! Not a single question to Nakul bhaiya..

After a while, Nakul bhaiya settles down. He takes a 1 rupee note from Amma and goes out. He receives a reward for bundling me out like a pile of torn clothes!

How would I ever forget this day? This moments of savagery will rankle me for a long long time

I will bounce back when I grow big and able

Scene transition

Days and months fly off

More than half of the students in our class shows remarkable improvement in English. If you take the Class, stand tall on its own is an elite group comprising a handful of frontbenchers. After a full 2 years of phenomenal struggle with the language, this elite group, which inclusive of me, upgraded itself from the rest and exhibits fine language skills, a cut above the rest of everyone. Seemingly Next Level Guys!

Alas! I still can't tame Maths. And I don't think, would ever be able to. Each passing day, hatred develops against Mr. Lucius Gabriel and his Maths. I hate him and will hate him forever. Even if that means, I never pass his subject in my entire curriculum!

Oops! I forget to tell you. As Mr. Lucius Gabriel puts it, I was short of 3 marks to pass in Maths in the last year finals, but I was given moderation, which helped me pass to Class VII. Besides, my overall average was good enough with excellent score in English, and above average in Chemistry and Social Studies

In fact, I must've been detained in Class VI if not for the stern support extended by my Ms. Theresa, who was happy with me for being the class toper in English. Though, in the process I surpassed her son, my best friend and classmate, Joyce by 2 marks, she was profoundly happy for me

On a later date, Joyce reveals, Ms. Theresa pleaded with Ms. Agnes and Mr. Lucius Gabriel to promote me. Eventually, Mr. Lucius Gabriel had to give his nod to help me pass with moderation mark in his subject. What actually transpired among the three, Joyce is not very sure, but am happy except for the fact that Mr. Lucius Gabriel is going to be our Maths teacher this year too. So..no reprieve from Mr. Lucius Gabriel. Am stuck and gasping for breath at the hands of Mr. Lucius Gabriel just the way a sea diver gets caught between the limbs of a dangerous Octopus; and it has Eight mantles!

It's no secret that Ms. Theresa has always been very kind and considerate to me. This was another classic example which stands testimony to her very special love and compassion for me as an individual representing such a noble profession

Scene transition

A week passes. I slowly come to terms with the horrid thrashing I suffered at the hands of Nakul bhaiya. It's late night. May be half past 10. All are asleep. I sink deep into my usual fancy thoughts. I jump into the cockpit to fly the aeroplane with glittering all white uniform ornamented with Gold and Black shoulder flaps and decorative cuff designs, when I suddenly hear from Amma and Appa. Appears to be something confidential, but what catches my attention is, Amma sounds uncharacteristically cool and composed. This is not familiar to me. Amma always has a dominant voice during family discussions. Some indistinct conversation flows into my ears..

'Nakul is asking a wrist watch, and get him the same model and brand he has shown in the magazine', Amma

'He is asking an expensive brand. I checked with the shop. Again, he put a full stop to his studies long ago. But Sanju is in Class VII. I think, we must pay more attention to him. Such an expensive watch for Nakul is an extravaganza now', Appa

'So what? He is my eldest child. Get it when you come tomorrow night. We can take care of Sanju's demands later', Amma's firm words

Long silence. Appa knows, Amma is argumentative, and win over her is as difficult as expecting the Biblical camel to pass through the eye of a needle. Pointless and impossible!

Ample evidence to prove that the relevance of my existence as her child, is further abused

Amma doesn't love me or what?

Why am I discriminated?

Am unable to sleep

Every day, whether in school or in my house, am subjected to severe emotional damage. My life is a zero..a big zero!

I lead a third rate boyhood life unworthy mentioning. There's something seriously wrong with my very being

How am I going to shape up my individuality and prove my worth to the world?

Amma doesn't care about my feelings and emotions. It remains an enigma. I feel a total Blackout. Don't know where my thoughts are driving me to. May be, she loves me, but doesn't want to showcase. May be because, she thinks, if she does so, Nakul bhaiya might envy. But then, what's such a big deal in that? We are her children. Came from her womb. We all should be equal in her eyes without any trace of bias

Does there exist some sort of bigotry?

Unable to make out. Can't logically conclude

As a 12year old, I can't reason it further

I tightly shut my eyes. No room for a fancy world tonight

In your dreams, you can be a daring warrior fleeing past in a chariot pulled by 7 snowy-white horses, but the real life is far from dreams; in fact, too far. But I can't help being a dreamy little boy, and I love dreams even if it means the most silly, but the enchanting of them all, may never come true! After all, I do not want to be a niggard in seeing dreams. Be too generous at least in my dream, I'm the glam-sham boy with a magic wand. Let my dreams remain dreams till my end. My pleasure!

Next day night. Am eagerly awaiting Appa's arrival. He comes around quarter to 9. He hands over a small pouch to Amma. He looks at me and he notices that am still awake

Nakul bhaiya and Somi are awake too

Granny is asleep. The moment she sees a piece of futon, she starts snoring

In the dim light of kerosene lamp, I get to see the watch while Amma unfurls the colorful wrapper. Rectangle shaped plastic box housing the beautiful Blue-dial steel wrist watch

Wow! It's a dazzling crafty piece. Cant' have a closer look

'Go to sleep Sanju, you've seen it and that's enough', Amma is irked by my bewildered eyes

Do I've an evil eye or what?! It's my curiosity, nothing else

My eyes filled. Can't exactly say what's flashing through my mind. Only I feel my renunciation. The pain of rejection and impoverishment. No one else can feel it or grasp it except my Granny, and due to age factor, she is no more strong-willed

'Come Nakul, it's yours', Amma invites Nakul bhaiya

Nakul bhaiya snatches it from Amma. He squeals in delight

There's one thing. Appa's face is cloudy. May be, he understands what am going through, but he is mentally fragile. Appa is grappling between contentment and loads of responsibilities, which make him vulnerable. But he tries to wear the temperament of a soldier who lost his composure long ago!

Though am only 12, I read his mind in many such occasions. He is not the type who throws his weight around. He is calm and receptive

Poor Appa! I love him without boundaries. If I get a second life on earth, I urge the Creator to be his son once again, but then, as his eldest son this time. Not the youngest!

I bury my face into the pillow trying hard to fight back my tears. For, if I cry aloud, Appa wouldn't sleep tonight. Night is wearing on, but still youthful and I've a long way to conquer!

Appa is polite and down to earth. Straight forward and much loving and caring of his children. We never see him crummy or atrocious, but very articulate. He is a Gem of a father. Even some of the Brat grownups in our locality respect him more than their own parents. With his scar-less persona and simplicity, he simply commands respect around!

Appa is jovial with everyone. He can crack a joke spontaneously, perfectly befitting the situation. Appa is the coolest father I get to see in the whole environs!

Scene transition

Another Monday morning. Amma is gearing up for a visit to her native

'Sanju, Amma is going to see our Maternal granny. She is sick. We've gotten the wire yesterday. Also, aunt's marriage is around the corner', Somi comes to me

'Is it'? Am gladly surprised as Amma wouldn't be around for 2 or 3 days. What a thrill!

'Yes, Appa is going to bus station to drop Amma', Somi

She too looks happy and relaxed. I can guess the secret behind her concealed joy. We both have the same reason to rejoice

'We can make merry in the coming days, in Amma's absentia', Am at the peak of excitement and can't control. My joy flows out

'I think so. We Three, Granny, and Appa', Somi

'We can have the time of our life without the hostel warden around', I make a sarcastic remark

'Fine, but if you roam around with your filthy tricks, I'll report to Amma when she gets back, remember', Somi cautions

'And she asked me to take care of you on your homework and studies. Also Am to keep a close tab on your activities', Somi

'Oh My God'! I exclaim, looking at her face agape. 'Is it so'? I verify

'Yes Sanju, exactly. Now, clear off. I've other works to finish', Somi

Somi takes intermittent breaks from school. She's not very keen in her studies. She cools off at home at her will. She has Amma's blanket approval for skipping school

She makes it to IX class this year with great hard work and a little bit of luck. She was at the brink of fence in total marks she scored in her final exams

I've nothing to be overwhelmingly cheerful about. Even my movements are under watch and scrutiny!

Appa leaves with Amma. She is carrying a small traveller bag stuffed with her personal clothing and some pleasantries for our Maternal grandma. Appa takes care of courtesies. He doesn't miss many

Here, Granny is still in bed. Not caring about Amma leaving for her native place

I go to her. Fondly oscillate her hollow earlobes. Both her earlobes hang loose like swings with more than1 inch diameter holes

'Your Grandpa got me heavy earrings made of pure British sovereign, you know little brat, huh'?

'How do I know those ancient details'? Am amused at her boasting. She heaps praises on my Grandpa off and on with no specific reason

None of her grandchildren has ever seen him. Even Appa who is the eleventh child of Granny reminisces sometimes that he has a vague single bit memory of Grandpa lifting overhead the last sibling, Appa's younger sister who is number 12. She is now living in a small town not too far from us. She has 5 children, all girls and 1 boy

However, Granny continues to claim that she had given birth to 11 daughters and 1 son, a total package of 12, which she couldn't prove so far!

She never gives a specific reply on what happened to her other 5 daughters. It remains a mystery!

This aunt intermittently visits her elder sister who is Appa's elder too, and lives in our neighbourhood. She however, seldom drops in at our house. It's a known secret among our relatives that Appa's sisters are not cordial with Amma

Granny's child number 12 comes recently to see her ailing older sister. She looks very humble and down to earth. She brings along her eldest daughter too. She is parallel to Nakul bhaiya age wise. Looks fair with a thin mane. Sharp chin frame with beautiful round eyes. She looks serious with a girl of few words. We didn't converse much. She acted a bit too much, trying to be my big cousin..of course, she's my big cousin. My aunt's daughter..

I once grow curious and ask Granny and Appa, 'what happened next, I mean after lifting my small little aunt atop his head? He slowly emancipates'? I taunt Granny in a lighter mood

'He boarded a ship and went across the deep ocean to work in the sugarcane forest, and never comes back'. That was his ill-fated journey'

Granny's voice dooms and diminishes. Her gloomy face tells it all. I never asked her that one question ever after!

Scene transition

It's half past 8 in the morning, and Am scurrying to Vibha's house. Already late

She is at the doorstep. Obviously, awaiting me

'You're too late', she screams

'There is a morning glad news Lilliputian. Amma has left for her parental house today morning. Our Maternal grandma is sick. Received a wire', I say

'But why are you late'? She is quizzing me. Not happy for me being late

'I think, today we go via the creek. Summer just got over, and there's no much water in the river. It has long ago dried up. Monsoon is only picking up. It will be real fun Vibha'

It was a flowing river once upon a time. It's now almost dried up with water pools and small river beds with African mosses floating on the top and mud filled bottom. There're quite a few sluggish spots. Some dry areas are used for paddy cultivation. It takes 15 minutes extra than our regular route to reach the school

'Come Ms. Dwarf. Don't say no Vibha'

'You've spoiled my plan', she doesn't want to stop

Vibha's nature is such. Small little things upset her. And it takes some time to subside

'What plan? Now, come with me as an obedient small little girl', I give stress to the last part

I pull her out of the room and take a few steps

The long sleeve of her typical school bag made of thick cloth sits pretty firm on her left shoulder, weighing her shoulder slightly down

Her school bag is almost of her length. My mood is to tease her, but I control. She is not in her usual self today as am late

We take the long walk along the river side. It's dried up in most of the places. Fast becoming a complete creek. But in some places, we can see rice crops sway in the air in both sides awaiting harvest. It's interesting to watch the harvesting done by labourers, a mix of men and women from the villages. There is a common dress code, which is unimposed. Colourful lungi and shirts with a cotton turban loosely fitted around the forehead by males and females alike. In our place, right from planting primed paddy seeds until harvest, activities are done manually. Tractor is a rare scene. The workers sing folk songs in chorus and crack facetious jokes. Maybe, it helps them forego their struggles for a moment. Songs are traditionally rhythmic and beautifully sung. Nobody ever compose the texts. It's a rural music that originally passes down to families and small social groups, enriched with oral tradition, generation after generation. How wonderful it is!

We cross the fields and come across a 2-meter long pot hole. It's a gap between paddy field and drainage ditch formed due to soil erosion during the current monsoon. The gutter is filled with sticky black mud occasionally. We must plunge inside to cross over. I look around for an alternate path. No other way out. This cleft was not found when we came a few months ago

I carefully step inside. There is mud well above my ankle level. I slowly let her in, hold her hand and inch forward. Though she lavishly rolls up her long uniform skirt, loose mud splashes up above her knee level. I don't want to be too adventurous. Carefully guide her forward. Must reach school in time. We struggle to move our feet wrapped in thick gluey mud. Feet are heavy. Finally we cross over, and another 10 minutes brisk walk, we are at our school gate. No water tap in this long stretch. I know

We hear the second bell. This means, teachers get alert and move to classes. We are damn late

I hold on to her right hand and run to the water tap just outside the gate. It takes another 5minutes to reach the school verandah

Vibha rolls up the stairs leading to her division

Thank God! Teacher has not come yet. Huge relief! I move ahead and occupy my corner seat at the front side row

Chapter 9

Another lucky day in the school gets over. Initial days of my class VII

In the evening, while returning from school, Vibha unfolds a tasty secret

'Sanju, Amma is preparing Unniyappam today evening. She asked me to invite you for the evening snack. And ya, with your favourite goat milk coffee. Amma specially asked me to take you along'

'Wow'! What a news!

Lakshmi aunt knows am very fond of Unniyappam. She ensures that I get a major share whenever she prepares it

My feet pick up pace at the very thought of soft steamy Unniyappam with goat milk coffee

'Come fast, my little baby girl', I lovingly pull her arm, suddenly, my affection is doubled

She notices it. Her big round eyes grow bigger in disbelief

'How could you keep it under wrappers for so long'? 'It's such a big news, do you know'?

'I wanted to give you surprise. And then, you were late in the morning, right'? She gently bites her lower lip, partially showing her upper teeth

Why girls make such cute gestures after committing serious lapses. May be, to compensate for the slip

Anyways, it's a very pleasant surprise from Vibha

'Don't pull me like that Sanju', she pleads

'Here's the punishment for you. Such a glad news you kept under wraps this long', I say half jokingly

'Now roll faster', I order. Can't wait any more to swallow Unniyappam. My stomach is ready with digestive juice

She looks at me yelling something very naughty

At last, when we reach her home, it's past 4.30. It's good that Amma had left for her parental house, and I can spend at least One hour at Vibha's

'Come Sanju', Lakshmi aunt invites me inside

I go to the backside, wash my hands and face. Make entry inside through the kitchen door

I can feel the aromatic smell of hot Unniyappam inside the house. I throw myself on to the undone wooden coat. It makes a creaky noise

'Careful Sanju', Lakshmi aunt warns. She is like that, always very caring of me

Raji brings me a plate-full of Unniyappam with Goat milk coffee in a half litre steel glass

I've the appetite to swallow an elephant. This plateful of Unniyappam poses no challenge for me!

I munch Unniyappam slowly while taking irregular sips of hot coffee. Impeccable experience. Golden chapter of my life!

Rare occasions when I feel am also someone to reckon with. Here, everyone makes me feel counted

Bharath is not visible

I feel excessively happy that someone on this planet earth gives me food and love without being toiled in return!

I finish the whole plate with ease

Take my notebooks and slowly get up from the cot. Don't feel like to part ways with this lovely hospitality

From the door, I turn back to Vibha. She smiles

Time is 6. I walk down

Scene transition

Next day. It's Tuesday. One of my favourite days. Tuesday has astronomical connections with Planet Mars. And Mars is not thought to be a planet with virtuous features. Many Pandits say, it's the Papgrah, means, the planet of sins. Though Mangal means auspicious, planet Mars is considered noxious. However, when I turn the pages of calendar ever since I can remember, am sure of one thing. Tuesday is a lucky day for me!

Amma is not there. Household affairs look cool and perfectly in place

Appa is humming his favourite age old film songs one after another. Am sure he hasn't seen those Black & White movies; probably, might have my Granny seen. Whenever Appa is humming a song, either he is filled with happiness or Amma is cooking some special dishes in the kitchen.

These are the two occasions when we get to see Appa humming a song

Appa's mood gives rise to some pleasant speculations. First, he may not go to shop today. Second, we can expect some rich mouth-watering cuisines at home with Granny as the Head Chef and Somi playing a second fiddle. Nakul bhaiya is not interested in cooking, but he eats. Am happy either way if Amma's prying eyes are not there after me doing spy work!

So, what's in store today?

Granny declares the program for the day

'You Bala', she fondly addresses her son, my Appa, 'don't go to work today. Kids will take a day break from school, strictly, and strictly no homework'

'We are not going to ask Sanju and Somi to open their books', Granny makes a big announcement about the package of entertainment bonanza for the day

Am immensely happy. Granny knows how to win hearts!

But how will I see Vibha? No big deal. After lunch, I sneak out and visit her. With Amma not around, there shouldn't be any obstacle, other than of course, Somi

So..here we go shopping. Granny, Somi, and me, myself, Sanju! Appa and Nakul bhaiya stay back

We've a small town, Kanjikuzhy nearby. In fact, our house is not far from the main town either, just two kilometres from bus stand or railway station

Kanjikuzhy isn't very small. We find all facilities here. It's a booming township..a main junction with good restaurants, beauty parlours, cool bars, department stores, toddy shop, fish and vegetable markets, sawmill, bakeries, flour mills, Bank, provision stores. We buy almost all things from Kanjikuzhy. Not too far from the hustle and bustle of the main town

I look at Granny. She is brimming with charm and enthusiasm. Any why not? She takes over as the Head of the Family till Amma makes her return. Somi and me know there's another secret behind Granny's new-found vigour. Granny drinks toddy. She has been having this habit before I was born. And now that she is the acting mistress of the family, nobody is going to stop her. She is going to manage the complete finance for the coming days

We reach near the toddy shop. This is popular in our town. Curries cooked here are known for its taste in farther places. There are many toddy shops near and far, known for their special cuisines. Appa would tell his friends about some specific dish, and his friends intercept taking the name of a certain outlet, which is famous for that dish. Every toddy shop has a signature dish of its own, which no other shop serves with the same lip smacking taste and texture!

Granny asks us to wait a few yards short of the toddy shop, in front of an Ayurveda medicines reseller, where consult is free, and medicines on payment. The doctor is too small in size physically and commands no respect at all from kids even. Me and Somi go inside showing no courtesy to the vaidya, and occupy 2random wooden stools. He looks at us with a familiar expression and turns to the passengers waiting at the opposite bus stop

'Don't go anywhere, be here', Granny

She then turns to her right. 'Have a look at them', Granny tells the vaidya. He smiles at Granny without showing his teeth. His bald head shines like a brand new stainless steel bowl!

She then crosses the road and goes inside the toddy shop. I see one drunkard at the entrance comes out. He dances in a gingerly manner and extends a raw village salute to Granny

True salute of a drunkard. A real comic scene clearly visible from here

Granny goes inside like a welcome guest and disappears somewhere. Obviously, any drunkard can in no way ill-treat Granny in Kanjikuzhy toddy shop. She is well-known in the locality and she commands by virtue of her age and her trademark open smile. Besides, Granny is known by Appa's stature and repute in surrounding places. Granny makes her presence impactful wherever she goes. She is crowd-pleasing

'It has been more than 15 minutes since Granny went inside, let's go and have a check', Somi suggests. She is not impressed with waiting for that long

'No. Granny asked us to stay here. Children are not supposed to go near a toddy shop. We'll wait another 10 minutes, I suggest

'Granny can't spend like this. Money Appa gives is for the expense of our family. I'll tell Amma when she comes', Somi sounds irritated with Granny's finance management

'Look Somi, don't be too smart. I'll tell Appa that you're sceptical about Granny's small little happiness. And you know, we are going to get my favourite fish, Granny promised me', I said

Am very happy. Rather, am happy with whatever Granny does today. I know, in the end, she'll make the day nice and delightful for all of us taking care of everybody's welfare. She has simple and flexible conditions to live life!

And, here appears Granny with a tailor-made smile on her lips. In fact, a smirk on her face making 2 big dimples more visible on her cheeks. She looks cool, but is dragging her feet if noticed keenly. Resembling the famous character Jean Val jean of Les Miserables coming out of the jail. Am sure, she has had a full bottle of Toddy

'Quality stuff', her expert comment

Somi gives me a double-meaning look

We walk down to the fish market

Granny knows my favourite fish. It's Pink Perch

'Come Sanju, we'll buy some vegetables. Let Granny look for fish', Simi calls

'Yes, come', I go with Somi. She takes a One rupee note from Granny and comes along

'Come on kids, what are you looking for'? Gracy, the vegetable vendor gives a wide smile. She sits on a tomato box converted as a makeshift sitting arrangement to keep her heavy frame. Given her physique, I don't think, the tomato box will last the whole day!

We buy some vegetables, a quarter-size piece of a coconut and turn back

'I got some fresh Pink Perch. Gopi charges a reasonable rate. He was very considerate when I asked for some 10 numbers. Nice guy', Granny is all praise about the fish vendor Gopi

He is our regular guy. When Granny comes to market, she goes to no one else

I notice, some shopkeepers apply pleasing techniques, and they display these techniques to woo customers using certain mannerisms

Here is this fish vendor, smiles to maximum limit; 2corners of his lips almost touch his both earlobes. It's my legitimate fear that one day; his lips will lose its elasticity and become stiff. But, remember, his smile is the only compliment you get. He charges too high. We normally don't buy from him

But again, someone rightly said, 'one who can't smile, shouldn't run a shop'

He just follows the proverb!

It's almost 12 noon when we eventually reach back home

Wow! My favourite fish fry and curry for lunch today. Come to think of it, I go literally insane. Pink Perch is my craze. I can simply feast on a full plate without break. My mouth is set to drool!

'Get some water Sanju, and help me with other chores', Somi's voice suddenly wakes me up

Nakul bhaiya is not seen around

Appa takes a nap. He seems tired or perhaps, feeling relaxed today

In the morning, I notice Appa's2-day old beard. A mix of salt and pepper. Not a right mix. Salt grains are more. He is ageing too fast. Appa never opens up. I never see him pouring his heart out to anyone. He defuses his emotions inside. His face tells it all!

I fill water in 2 big storing vessels. Now, it's easier for them to use

The 2 chefs are busy in the kitchen working hard

After a while, I make a flash visit to kitchen. Rice is boiling in the big earthen pot. I open the top lid. Brown rice is boiling making big bubbles on the surface

Bubbles burst and form again in clusters

'Sanju, just check whether the rice is cooked. It shouldn't turn to mush. Take the big ladle, not the flat paddle, Somi

'And be careful. Don't burn your fingers', she adds

I put the big Aluminium ladle in the rice and give a good stir. Scoop some rice in the ladle and squeeze

'Ouch', I scream. It's very hot

'Leave it and go. I'm done with you joker. This is why Amma doesn't allow you inside kitchen. You can't properly manage even small little things', Somi comes running in for my rescue

Somi is right. Amma never allows me inside kitchen. She says, am too curious to check half-cooked dish and make premature opinions. In our home, no one enjoys the right to make a passive comment on the quality of food Amma cooks, obviously!

I give them a slip and come out. Eager to have lunch. This occasion doesn't come every day. Feel extremely happy

I spread the mattress. Feeling hungry. Lie down flat on my stomach. This is what I do when am hungry

Yummy aroma of fried fish swirl inside the room, not spreading out of the room. This smell enthrals me more than anything. The smell of tasty, rich food! The feel is simply awesome. I get up and sit flat ready to eat

Time is passing slowly. Can't sit. I gently lie down supine and shut my eyes..

'Go Sanju, wash your face and come. Lunch is almost ready. Wake up Appa and look for Nakul bhaiya, he must be there around', Granny's pleasant voice stirring up my appetite from the bottom of my stomach

I bounce up like a Tennis ball

Appa gets up without being woken up. Nakul bhaiya is not very impressed with what's happening in the kitchen

'Sanju, call Nakul', Appa

I come out hesitantly. Nakul bhaiya is giving a patient hearing to his friend Jotiprakash. Some curious talk. Joti, we fondly call him, is a close friend of Nakul bhaiya. Joti possesses high self-esteem. He is the 'good boy' of our locale

Amma likes him very much. Whenever special meal is prepared, Amma makes it a point to invite Joti

Nakul bhaiya invites Joti for meals, but he says no, and leaves for some urgent work

Nakul bhaiya enters. He doesn't speak much to me after that incident when he caned me mercilessly the other day

I don't like facing him either. He is a cruel sadist, way ahead of Mr. Lucius Gabriel

Somewhere in the afternoon. I run to Vibha's

Her house is locked. I look around

Where have they gone?

Why hasn't she informed?

Why? Why? Why?

I come back desperate

I was very happy a little while ago, but see how the destiny shapes the things around me!

My plan to meet Vibha is doomed to a total disappointment. Short-lived happiness I always have. Almighty doesn't want to see me happy and in peace a little too long. Am not fortunate enough to have what my heart desires

The night is mysteriously silent. Granny is not in her usual self. She is tired. Might be, the day's tiresome activities have taken a toll on her. Am preparing her day's last beeda, grinding betel leaf with areca and a small amount of tobacco and lime. I've a small portable grinding stone exclusively for grinding her preparation. Her regular prescribed quota is 3 or 4 times. Granny doesn't like anyone else do it, other than me. I won't too let anyone hijack this right from me!

I take so much pride in being her most favourite grandkid. Granny has only 6 daughters now alive and my Appa is her only son, the Eleventh

Beeda is ready. I squeeze the mix in my right hand to make it further soft, and take it near to her mouth. This is the routine we both maintain since am 4 or 5 years old. I make the preparation and carefully plant it inside her mouth. Granny's mouth opens straight up instinctively as though her jaw is fitted with an automatic scent sensor

Her mouth always smells fresh betel leaf and the smell is not at all displeasing

Another day comes to a close. Am not peaceful as I couldn't see Vibha today and more to that, her house was found locked

I struggle to pass 2 days. Perhaps because I can't get to see Vibha. Am going through a turmoil. Am restless. I must know where have they gone. And why Vibha did fail to inform me before leaving

Next day, I check with Ramesh in the school during recess. He is Vibha's cousin brother. Their mothers are biological sisters

'Hey Ramesh, where's Vibha'?

He stops after a few steps farther

'Why? What happened'? Displeasure largely writ in his tiny eyes. I know, Ramesh is not very pleased with our harmony

'Tell me where's Lakshmi aunt, Vibha? Where've they gone? Their house's locked', am impatient

'What's the matter'?

'I prepared some notes for Vibha. I wanted to give her', I lied

'I too have some doubts, Ramesh

'Say chapter and contest', I say

'From the book Huckleberry Finn. Would you help me too'?

He is framing conditions

'Yes, of course'

No options. He plays his game cleverly not only in the field. Bloody clever wolf. Who knows him better?

'They're off to see our eldest aunt. She's sick'. They may be back tomorrow

At last a breakthrough! I sigh

Ramesh walks away

Chapter 10

Today morning Amma comes back. She looks very happy. Her younger sister's marriage is fixed with a local guy. He owns a workshop of metal framing and welding works. I overhear Amma explain details to Appa. Amma when speaks family details, is very careful of not letting her voice falling into any silly guy. She keeps her voice to minimum decibel! After all, am nothing short of an outsider!

I've serious doubts, whether am filled with enough ounces of confidence, which a boy of my age supposed to be having. At times, I feel some crucial links missing, some vital cords that are essentially akin to my emotional inner wellbeing

I must study well. Find a job in a farther place. A place where my troubled childhood shouldn't be haunting me any further. I will go. And never to return! Don't want to be a mere option in anybody's life! My thoughts are intertwiningly occupying my mind. Not a haven of relief or shelter anywhere soon. Am at the budding stage, and will bloom into an adorable flower with adorable soft petals and enchanted fragrance spreading everywhere. But yes, there is a long journey to complete before I reach my goal

Time and tide never waits. No one can control, stop, or deflect it's course. It's a universal phenomenon!

I withdraw more and more into myself locking me inside a shell like the one of a cocoon. It's heart-wrenching, but I love this solitude. It's self-imposed!

Maths continues to be the wrecker-in-chief among all subjects. Every time, my scorings in Maths tests go from bad to worse inflicting irreparable damage to my morale. I get shameful numbers in this subject, not touching double figures most of the times..

What if I don't pass this year? I no longer get good sleep. Losing focus in English too. My scores in the last 2 class tests hit an all-time low. Am in sixth or seventh spot now's. Theresa is not happy at all. She gives me a mouthful in the middle of the whole Class

'You're getting complacent Sanju. Don't think you are invincible and shall ever remain on top. All the top 5 guys have made remarkable improvement. They shocked me even', Ms. Theresa

I understand, she mocks at me for finishing a paltry seventh position in the last concluded mock test before the finals

Can't digest it anymore. 'I..I..will teacher', I mumble. I feel stiff constraints to face the Class

'What I will..? My foot. If you've the potential, prove it in your performance and show to the Class. Don't be in a fool's world, Sanju'

Oh My Goodness! She has not yet stopped!

Scene transition

Something glides to my mind out of contest. It was in class V. We are all new, no much acquaintance to each other. A few months gone by, on a dull afternoon, Physics teacher, Mr. Ganapathi walks in for Science class as usual

He isn't happy with me, I know. He surely hasn't forgotten my below par performance in the very first class test in his subject. My score was something which he would have never expected. Till then, he had carried the impression that am good at his subject!

Later, he was on leave, 5 days or so..

This break was a small hiatus, but not enough a reason to cause anyone severe Amnesia!

'Turn to page 13, Chapter 4, come to the last but one paragraph. Read louder', Mr. Ganapati roars to me

'The topic is about buoyant force. Do you remember Sanju'? Mr. Ganapati roars again

Mr. Ganapati has a high decibel voice as loud as a lion. The Headmistress' office must have gotten alerted!

Am confused. There's lack of clarity in my mind. Can't clearly make out his instructions though it's distinctly given. Everyone is ready with the page, but am not. Still searching for the page and paragraph

Am blinking. No clues, but still keep flipping the pages hurriedly like a lunatic

I try to peep into Joyce' text book

He understands, and am obliged

Oops! Finally, am able to track the exact page and paragraph. Courtesy, Joyce' benevolence

Mr. Ganapati looks impatient

'Yes sir, I remember. You explained it in the last classes, I reply confidently

'Now, C'mon. Explain Buoyant force', Mr. Ganapati

'Buoyant force is the upward action or the pressure exerted by a fluid towards an object to float', I look at him smartly

'Fair enough', sit down, Mr. Ganapati. He acts as though he is granting me unconditional bail in a criminal case

I look around jubilantly and settle down. Am elated

Mr. Ganapati went on to explain further about Buoyant force

What makes something float or sink? He connects Buoyant force to Archimedes' principle. He brings in a fair amount of Maths to Physics formulae and makes it almost look like Maths

This is the one thing I hate in Mr. Ganapati. Otherwise, I've a 'scratch my back - I will scratch yours' attitude towards Physics. I don't find any harm learning it either!

He also teaches with supportive learning activities using tools and utensils. When 'Buoyant force 'was in full force, school Housekeeping staff Ms. Mary was summoned with a bucket of water. It was kept in the middle of the class. Mr. Ganapati very quickly makes some paper boats and let it float on the surface of water

We all throng encompassing the bucket. Mr. Ganapati was caught in the hustle, and was pushed to the middle. He was caught in the rush and panic of the force exerted by the exterior human force applied collectively. He makes a nosedive into the bucket of water. We at first, were shocked and then suddenly, the whole class laughs the heart out!

Thank God! The stampede knocked down the bucket too right in time, and Mr. Ganapati comes out unscathed. But what happened looks straight from a comic opera!

Scene transition

Evening, back home without Vibha. Another day elapses without having her company. My wavering starts surfacing out. Granny smells something fishy

'Are you hooked up with someone'? Granny asks me sarcastically, and then, she suddenly breaks into a hearty laugh

She tries to be facetious. Absolutely harmless joke

'Granny, don't be stupid'. I warn her. I seldom get serious with Granny

My response doesn't go well with her. Perhaps, I stupefy her with my artificial arrogance

The only soul that breathes for me. In return, I prepare her betel mix 3- 4 times a day!

'Oh leave it granny', I console her and run out without caring for the sagging branch of my Mulberry tree. I rammed into it hurting my forehead 'oucchh', I feel the pain hard and almost fall down losing my gait

'Child, careful', Granny

She comes running and sits on the muddy ground. There is laceration and swelling on my forehead

She gently runs her fingers over the minor gash. Blows out warm air. Her breath fresh betel leaf

'It's Summer and you should be careful my darling child. Don't hurt yourself as the season is bad. You will aggravate your wound', Granny spills her general knowledge in Medical Science

Granny has always been like that. She comes up saying, 'it's the wrong season and you can't afford to get hurt at this time as the weather is bad'. So, according to Granny, literally, one can't get hurt any time of the year!

To her, all seasons are bad and will aggravate your wounds!

Obviously, you can't reason with Granny, for if you discredit her expertise, you will end up annoying her. She being a super senior citizen with abundant knowledge and experience in life, it's not prudent to argue with her

'Take a day off from school', Amma's generosity

'Not interested', I said

I don't want anyone's sympathy

Suddenly, her affection flows out..why?

'Do what you feel like', Amma murmurs and retires from the scene, not very happy seeing me resting my head on Granny's laps

'You spoil my child, pampering him too much. He is grown up now', Amma doesn't forget to issue a stern warning to Granny before she backs off

'Your son is past 16. Why don't you stop pampering him? In Sanju's case, I still have a good 3 years to spoil him. What about your son?', Granny retorts

'You have spoiled him beyond correction, and you just don't care', Granny fires another salvo

'You are encouraging Sanju by criticising his elder brother. Mind it', Amma

Granny refers to Nakul bhaiya as 'your son', when she locks horns with Amma where am involved

It's Granny's expression of strong resentment against Amma on my distress. Granny construes, Amma is discriminative. Not fair with me

'No such things. I just try to separate grain and the chaff', Granny looks very angry. She is sweating due to mental exertion

'Will you keep quiet?', Amma losing her cool

'You subside then. You sowed the seeds of hatred among your children', Granny almost removes the pin from the grenade. This is getting curious and may seriously ruin the peace of our family

The argument continues..

Chapter 11

Final exams just got over. Am not very optimistic about Maths. My record has been dubious throughout this year. Not very hopeful to get through

Somewhere in the midst of Summer vacation. It's our keen discussion about kite flying. This is very popular during the next big festival. It's months away though. This festival is the biggest celebration time at par with Christmas, Ramzan, or Baisakhi. Most popular hobby during this festival is kite flying. Among boys, it's the most sought after game in our place.

For adult men and women, it's Tug of War. This is probably the biggest game, for it lifts your spirit and vigour beyond boundaries. The classic climax it generates towards the end is unmatched. Physically strong team wins in this game, is the general concept. One could see an array of bodybuilders in both sides of the rope. But in addition, there are some tricks to win. Experience plays a major part. Plant your feet firm to the ground as your posture, and your grip on the rope shouldn't slip from the original position. Use your leg muscles to the maximum. Immediately start pulling the rope backwards. Don't waste a second, or else you will run out of steam. No time to think. It's not a technical game. A single tug of war game lasts for a few minutes only. Some are over within a minute. It all depends on team composition and their skills, and of course, physical strength

Special kind of thin colourful paper sheets available in shops during the season, twine, gum, and dry coconut leaf sticks. Travel from place to place, and you get to see different types of kites with style and elegance suiting the culture and diversities of that particular place. We make simple and beautiful traditional kites entirely different from the ones we see during big kite festivals in Jaipur or Ahmedabad. Bow and arrow made with dry coconut leaf sticks makes the main body frame that keeps the kite stiff. This is further fused with crafty designs in the anterior visible from both sides. Then fitted with designer paper tales on three sides of the square-shaped body leaving the top free of any attachment. This top edge works as a nose cone like that of a fighter jet. This sharp end enables the kite to cruise in the sky fast and vertically upward. Bow and arrow attached to the body pierced and knotted at the rear side which then connected to a roll of twine. You must be an adept to win the competition as to whose kite goes up in the sky to the highest and lasts long without any technical snag including a majestic landing at the end!

In our place, August – September is predominantly kite season as this part of the year marks the beginning of festival season

'Sanju am with you. Take me too to the school ground', Atchu books his birth well in advance

Atchu refers to the school where we study up to Standard IV. Tile roofed with only one entrance, and an exit at the opposite

It has a small levelled ground at the rear side, where brief programs and flag hoisting are conducted on Independence Day and Republic Day. If you scale the rear boundary wall, you get the main bus route connecting the famous Catholic Church and Kanjikuzhy town and beyond. Across this main road, one can see government bungalows for The District Collector, RDO, IPS Officers, and may be a few bungalows accommodating senior officials at the Department of Postal and Telegraph

We normally use the frontage ground. This can't be called a playground. There are bumps and pits everywhere with occasional tiny rock towers. Mowing of grass happen during annual sports competition. Some student athletes fall and fracture their knees and elbows on this ground during sports. But we don't care about wounds or sprains. Only one object in front, that's the opponent. Third and fourth standard students of this Lower Primary school run like professionals on this dangerously bumpy ground to win prizes. Winner will take home a plastic soap box or a thread and needle box or a bathing soap, which most probably may not be your regular brand. To earn these coveted prizes, we run fastest and jump highest and longest at the competitions as if it's our last chance before death. I had falls and got hurt on this ground many times during sports events

When the District Education Officer visits this school, there is a general assembly. We would stand in the hot sun making snake-like straight queues and listen to the Headmaster who nears retirement

Once, during DEO address in a General Assembly, somewhere in the middle of his speech, he happens to see this small little girl of Second standard who was sitting on a bench with her right forearm in plaster with supportive sling. She gets exempted from standing in the assembly and could sit on a bench when the DEO is addressing the students, makes him curious

After the small crispy speech of no much significance, the DEO approaches the little girl,

'What happened child'?

The girls was excited seeing the big bald man stands near

'I had a fall on this ground during the recent sports competition', she replies politely

'Which standard you belong to'? DEO

'Second standard', the little girl

'You are not supposed to participate in running competitions. That is for Third and fourth standard children', DEO turns back and looks at the Headmaster with a big question mark on his face

In this school, which has a facility only up to fourth standard, students from classes 1 and 2 are not allowed to be a part of running competitions. Considering their tender age and the pathetic condition of the ground, which looks susceptible to cause injuries to the school's budding athletes, school management follow this ruling since long ago

DEO is well aware of this constraint

Headmaster shyly approaches him with cold feet like a new bride stepping into the bridegroom's house

'Sir, she has a poor memory. The other day, she was playing during leisure hours and stumbled upon a Touch-me-not. The thorny stems did the trick. She didn't participate in running competition', Headmaster explains

The DEO looks at him suspiciously

'How come a small little girl of hardly 7 years could have cooked up such a false story'? DEO looks puzzled

Headmaster stares at DEO like a retarded person. His nervous eyeballs roll from corner to corner. No way, he could reveal that small children also run like horses in this ground, for want of participants during sports events

'Any way, take care of these tiny tots. I'll arrange to get necessary funds sanctioned for cleaning work of the entire school compound', his regular sweet box to the headmaster, which never comes true!

DEO leaves and the whole battery of teaching staff follow the suit with a huge relief

I was in fourth standard, my final year in this school. Till I left this school and joined the present seminary school in the city, I couldn't see any conservancy work happening here

Every year, during festive season, we come here to fly kites, and we see the ground more bumpy with more pits all around, and of course, with more Touch-me-nots grown up almost everywhere!

Atchu's whistle startles me. He applauds at the boys playing football just a few yards away. Looks like a new team. They don't belong here

Here, I see another boy, not from my friends' group comes. He hesitantly smiles

I signal him to come closer with my left hand fingers. A stout boy with round eyes. He should be eight or nine. I know him. Living slightly far from my neighbourhood

'Hello', I greet him, stretching forward my right hand for a shake keeping my palm inwardly parallel to the ground

'Hello bhaiya', he reciprocates with a smile. White teeth. Smile is good. May be, because he has a dark complexion

'You make kite for him, his demand. He has been waiting', Atchu explains

'Come here', Udhay looks at the boy, 'what is your name'?

'Vishnu', but the boy would not move his feet

The new entrant in our gang looks uncomfortable, for Udhay's arrogance doesn't go well with him

Udhay has a dim complexion, taller than me, and is overly built with female body features. He is not a welcome friend among our group members. He bullies other boys and has rowdy-like temperament. He strikes filthy altercations with unknown people. He is a clever guy and wouldn't give straight answer to a question. Not a regular school goer. Richer than all of us. His father runs a small-time business of handbags and consumer goods

He eats like a glutton. When 1 egg is a luxury for most of us, he gets to eat 2 eggs with breakfast. I see many times. He is a rude guy with the hostile attitudes of an adult

I don't like to keep his company, but try not to discard him from our activities

He is the potential villain on any given day. We all are aware of it. He simply picks up an argument with anyone anywhere. He just doesn't care about behavioural manners. Being the gang leader, I reprimand him some times for his obstinate conduct, but he doesn't care much. Udhay makes the Artful Dodger of our gang!

'I will make one for you', I assure Vishnu

'Let's sit closer'

'As usual, kite flying competition. Am with Sanju', Atchu reiterates his support to me as always

'We too', Suresh and Sunil make a joint statement

All 3 are my reliable, time-tested peers-cum-assistants

'Am with you', Vishnu

'Ramesh, this Udhay is your strength', Udhay boasts looking at Ramesh

Other than Udhay, Ramesh will enjoy the support of Siva, his closest neighbour but older than us. Vibha's younger brother Bharath would also support Ramesh, for they're close relatives and rather cousin brothers being children of biological sisters

Now the team composition is finalized. Two teams with four members each with Vishnu as common lieutenant. Any one from either of the team if doesn't make it on that day, Vishnu will take his place as substitute

While making kite is a tricky art, flying a kite is even trickier. It requires some technical acumen and patience to win the competition. If your kite has technical flaws, it won't fly and ascend in the air. Kite should stay balanced in the air while up in the sky and should oscillate evenly on both sides or else the kite will not get lifted further up in the air. After it gains good height, it doesn't require any manoeuvring. It can simply stand still without a shake

We disperse for the day, and I go back home

'Where were you Stooge'? Amma roars at the entrance. 'You are looking like a desi wrestler straight from action', she adds up

'Errrhh..', I search for words, want to throw some excuse

'How dare you have gone without my permission'?

Amma is in no mood to listen while am still composing something in mind. It's not easy to pacify the other person when he or she basically dislikes you

'Cleanse your hands and legs and come inside. I will put an end to your whims and follies today. It's on the rise', Amma

I feel a chill down my spine. She never excuses me. Not even once in my memory. Amma is like a fighter jet. Make one single mistake, and it crashes before you can even eject yourself!

Nakul bhaiya is not seen anywhere. He is like a seasonal guest. Comes and goes per his choice

Where's Somi? I look around, not seen

Granny sits in her regular couch and stare at infinity through the peep hole occurred from the damage of the main door. This hole has recently become bigger as the door is too old. Granny's flighty posture suggests that she is in discomfort

A miracle awaits me inside, I didn't know

After a good wash, I fit me into a pair of domestic clothes. Groom my hair with fingers. Present myself to Amma

'You called me..', I stop abruptly

'Eat this and fill your stomach. I know you are always hungry', Amma

She hands me a half-plate with Puttu and bananas. Another favourite dish of mine

I committed a big offence and Amma is cool! I can't believe this. It seems, the world is coming to an untimely end!

I gently look at her face. She looks tired. Our financial hardships take a toll on her. I never get to see Amma cheerful and happy other than certain rare occasions

I slowly go into the kitchen. Scan all plates and other serving cutleries

Amma doesn't have anything to eat

She observes what am doing

'Have you eaten anything, Amma'? My concern fills her eyes

I sit on the floor. Mix Puttu with banana

'Eat Amma', I said

She takes 1 or 2 fist-full, and then tenderly pushes the plate back to me

Amma's out of the blue gesture moves me. I can't sleep tonight, this time for an entirely opposite reason. Is Amma kind or cruel? Too many questions surface to top, but am not equipped to find the right answers. Or, my answers are incorrigible!

Chapter 12

It's a fine Sunday morning. I come out. Standing aimlessly under our Mulberry tree brushing my teeth. My toothbrush action has no strategic significance. First and foremost, it's a boring daily routine, additionally, a matter of personal hygiene, nothing else

I suddenly see Suresh appear in front with a broad wicked smile. His complete set of '32' almost visible

'Yes Suresh, anything'?, I quipped wearing an am-not-interested look on my face. Am seeing his face after a long, precisely, after he disappeared from the scene of Nakul bhaiya's savage assault on me. Being in different schools, we don't get to meet each other often. He helps his father in their shop till late in the evening and gets back home somewhere at night hours. It's the weekdays' routine of Suresh and Sunil

No wonder, am not impressed seeing his face now

We study in different schools. But he is my close friend. His father runs a shop in Kanjikuzhy

'Sanju, come to playground, Atchu and Ramesh await you', Suresh

He not at all looks like someone who just recently threw his friend to a lion's cage and ran away for the sake of own life. And now, he acts innocent like an infant. Bloody traitor!

'Get the hell out of here. You and Sunil could have done something to save me from his clutches', I can't hide my anger. It's my nature. What's in my mind will reflect on my face. No disguise

'Forget that. My Amma is cooking Sunday special today. It's your favourite. Sunil is off to Kanjikuzhy in the morning'

'Join us for lunch, Sanju. Now, c'mon man, cheer up'. He pulls my hand

'You know, Nakul bhaiya is a rogue. He is a wretched character. Who'll confront an incoming train inside a dark cave? Tell me. No ill-feelings, Sanju please', Suresh

I give it a thought. Analyze the deal's pros and cons. His invitation is not a bad bargain. Good proposal. I weigh it before saying yes

I had Sunday lunch in his home before too. It's worth paying a visit

It's always prudent to convert grievances into an asset. My wisdom tells me

'Kay, wait'. I quickly wash my petite face. Run In. Stand in front of the looking mirror. Apply a thick coat of Exotica on my skinny face

It's always been a challenge combing my hair. It's puffy, feather like. Just like tumbleweeds. Why comb, I can set it with my fingers!

Nakul bhaiya has thick flowing hairs. Fairer than me tall and flashy guy. Our neighbouring pretty girls make passes at him. I notice many times, but he doesn't bother. His friends had advised him to have a latest trend Step cut hairstyle, and now, he mills around with this hairstyle flaunting his flowing shiny hair. I would say, luck written all over his flesh and veins!

Amma pays for his luxuries. The tag of being the eldest son comes with lot of goodies, is not it? At least, in his case

'Hello, what sup man'? Somi's sudden appearance awakens me

Somi has a cat's paw. She suddenly appears from nowhere, but most of the time, to play the role of an infiltrator

'Where're you off to so early in the morning'?

'Quit the place'. I warn her, 'or else, am going to hit you'

'Let Amma come. I will get you'

'Give way, you crap', I shout

I no more like Somi and Nakul bhaiya. Hostility develops within me for my elder siblings. I constantly feel the changes happening in me

Relationship among siblings is unique, incomparable

I see Nakul bhaiya entering inside

Where has he gone in the morning so early.., am thinking

'Get to studies', order from Nakul bhaiya. The supreme command

'Kay', I recede signalling Suresh to leave

Nakul bhaiya makes a grinding noise, goes out and comes in a trice. I'm done with him, my God!

Bhagvati aunt lives in my close neighbourhood at the rear side. She has 7 children, all males. They've emotionally charged sentiments to each other. No outsider taunts them. Their connection has strong, intense bondage. Very closely-knit unit. Younger ones are found among the company of older ones playing and having fun together

We're only 3 siblings. Yet, unable to get along cordially

Neighbourhood friends of Bhagvati aunt crack jokes on her family population

'You are 9 members in your family and quite simply make a handsome political party in itself'

Bhagvati aunt is not the one to take things easy

'You too can form a political party in your house my dear, a larger group', she would retaliate

Siblings know each other, the scent of their sweat and warmth of their breath more deeply than their own parents who give them birth

I came across an article featured in a regional weekly some time ago. Siblings play dominant roles in one another's lives that simulate the camaraderie of parents and influence their lives to a farther extent. For the reason that, siblings generally grow up in the same household and background, and they've a substantial amount of exposure to one another. Very true!

Also, very pertinently, the influence and assistance of close friends play noteworthy roles too, but am short of too many friends either!

Look at Suresh and Sunil. Sunil is 3years younger to Suresh. They've a very strong connection. They've a younger sister also. Lovely siblings

Are my siblings too feeling same what I feel? No answers now. May be, one day, I will have!

'Come Sanju', Granny

Still sitting pretty cool on her old futon bed. Granny has no tooth as said earlier. No toothbrush. How simple and simplified her life is!

I go and sit near her

'Granny, coffee', Somi hands her a glassful of Black coffee

'Want to have Sanju'? Somi's benevolence

'No. Am going to Suresh's', not much interested in her coffee

Somi quits

'Beware, Nakul is watching', Granny's piece of advice. I know it carries weight

'Wait, will find some trick to help you sneak out. I will send Nakul to shop to get me Betel nuts'; Granny's idea sounds not too bad

Granny drinks hot coffee sip by sip very slowly enjoying every drop of it. Her pattern of eating and drinking is not similar to others. Irrespective of the food's consistency, she flattens the stuff inside and punches it with the roof of her mouth and swallows it in one stroke. No chocking. The food simply flows down her oesophagus without causing a slight obstruction. If closely watched, one can see granny does it with much ease. It's a sheer joy to watch the whole process!

'You Nakul', Granny calls out

'Granny', Brother Nakul appears as an obedient disciple

Against all odds, he respects Granny and showcases his love to her when he is in need of coins. Granny knows his weakness

Granny slowly unties the tight knot at the corner end of her dhoti from the hip. She has hard uncut nails, which look soiled. I must trim her nails today. It looks shabby, I think

'Go to the shop and get me Betel nuts and some tobacco', she hands a couple of 50-paise coins to Nakul bhaiya

'Keep the balance', tip from Granny

Nakul bhaiya pushes off

I stretch my neck out to see his current location. He is diminishing from the sight. He'll take at least 15 minutes to come back

'You sneak out. I'll manage Nakul', Granny's assurance

I gently step outside with a cat's paw without being noticed by Somi

Jogged to the field where my friends wait

I love playing with my friends like any other boy does. Our normal playground is a vast locale of dry land down the street. Everyone on the street knows each other. It's a lovely place to grow up. People come here for morning exercise. Men and women from the elite class come here in White Ambassador cars with Topiwala Chauffeurs who park the cars in a corner and take a fag. Among them, there's is this chauffer who stands out with his looks and Ivory white uniform. His poster resembles an evergreen hero of our regional language. Alas! The Hero had an untimely death though!

However, Amma doesn't like me play outside so much. She wants me at home where she could keep a spy eye on me for some ambiguous reasons. It sounds strange. May be, she has her own defence beyond logics. She forbids me from playing with friends. This is moulding into a severe obstacle in injecting adequate self-esteem and confidence in me!

Chapter 13

Time flies. Especially, when it's vacation time

I easily sail through Class VII final exam. Going to be in High school. Score good marks in all subjects, but just scrape through in Maths and regional language

Vibha too makes it with ease having just made the cut in English and without much fuss in other subjects

School is reopening today after vacation. Since am going to be in high school from this year, Amma had promised me to get regional newspaper from this academic year. I rope her in during the vacation itself. She's reluctant to dish out somewhere around Eleven rupees a month for a daily, which she says after all, only a paper. Old newspaper doesn't fetch you much either!

'On the other hand, when I give away Eleven rupees a month to Sreedhar, the Paperwala, it's a huge sum', Amma tries to counter my argument

'But from this year, am in Class VIII and it's important for me to be in touch with General knowledge and current affairs. What's the use of being a mere student, if am not in line with the latest updates on what's happening around? There is a lot of stuff to learn from the newspaper. It's not a luxury. A necessity for being a bright student', I argue

'Kay, inform Sreedhar. He'll issue us the number one regional daily in the country from June 1, the day your school reopens', Amma finally succumbs

No one buys newspaper in my close neighbourhood. Hence, we become the first household in our 'region' to have a Daily, and am on the top of the world for being a part of the Elite category!. Having daily newspaper is a mark of prestige and quality life, and it augurs as a symbol of being rich and well-to-do!

June 1. In these parts, it's a never-changing custom that it rains today morning, exactly at the time when we leave for school. It's like a Thumb rule. Sky's dark with thick clouds all around. We normally brave small little showers, but I must share the umbrella with Somi in case of a heavy downpour. Both of us are not keen in sharing a single umbrella, may be, owing to our state of incapacitation to gel with each other

'I'll get you a new umbrella next week', Appa's promise to me

Appa's promise normally ends up a huge disappointment, for he makes a commitment and forgets soon after

In fact, umbrellas and Appa have a strangely waggish connection. On a rainy day, he carries the umbrella with him but comes back without one, fully drenched in the heavy rain

'Where's the umbrella you had carried in the morning'? How could you awfully forget it when it's still raining? It's disgusting', Amma would confront

'I forgot that I had carried umbrella in the morning', Appa would reply with a trace of remorse

However, Appa keeps doing the same every season

And one fine day, Amma imposes a Life ban on Appa for use and carry of umbrella from home

I pick the umbrella and run to get milk with Suresh along. On the way, I can meet Sreedhar and get our newspaper straight from his hands rather than waiting for him till he comes for local area distribution. One more reason, if I go and get it, I can have a run-down through the newspaper before I leave for school. In that case, I would've been better equipped with the latest news updates and can score against the so-called intellectuals of the class when they come armed with updated minds during recess. I can have some shield of the latest buzz against them. This could be a fine technique to impress the Class on the very first day!

On a different note though, I can enjoy Phantom and Mandrake comics appear in this particular daily. I love comics; especially, Phantom who wears a skull ring, and punches his enemies leaving a skull mark on their cheeks. Reading comics regularly will help improve your language skills, I hear from Joyce. The practice helps you considerably get thorough with communicative English

Another matter of great interest, Wimbledon Tennis Championship starts in June. We don't have the luxury of watching TV, but can have exclusive sports news from the daily. Sports reporters of this print have real stuff. I keep a close tab on sports events happening across the globe and am sure about the participant players from our country representing each sport every year. Names of current list of champions and runners-up of any sports and games is in my finger tip

Wimbledon Tennis is one such area of mine with lots of passion. My favourite player's Bjorn Borg, the ice man. He wears a headband. Looks rock-solid throughout the entire game

But then, there's John McEnroe. While Bjorn Borg is professionally skilled, McEnroe is naturally talented and a strong hard-court player. A genuine Southpaw. Throws tantrums in the middle of the game, some times. Both're great players. I think, both should clash the finals. Definitely miss TV action live

But for patriotic reasons, I love to see Vijay Amritraj get past the Quarter Finals and play the Semis with may be, Ivan Lendl, the Czech-American or the South America Guillermo Vilas who is an another powerful lefty..

Among women, some all-time big names have lined up again this year. Zina Garrison, Tracy Austin who is the current US Open Champion, Chris Evert. Any of these may win the championship

Glory to God! Got the newspaper approval from Amma..

It's only 7 in the morning; expectedly, heavy downpour starts with storm. If it halts before 8, no need to share umbrella with Somi. She is in Matric this year. She had a test by fire in last year exams. She will have a real tough time this year!

We fetch milk from a slightly distant neighbourhood. The owner is a senior citizen, retiree from Federal Bank. His daughter-in-law is the matron of all his domestic and small-time business affairs inclusive of sale of milk, butter, cow dung, and vegetables from their kitchen garden. Moncy, his only son once says that his wife is managing his father's pension too. Understandably, Moncy failed to impress his father all his life. And how could he? Moncy is still unemployed!

Paper agent, Sridhar isn't seen anywhere. It looks, he found shelter somewhere and will come out of the den only after the rain recedes

Back home, am already late for bathe. Must be fast and take Vibha along. She passed with good marks, I hear from her younger brother Bharath

Huge disappointment on the very first day. Vibha is not coming due to a nasty stomach muscle cramp, which she suffered yesterday while playing Kho-Kho in her courtyard. What prompted her play Kho-Kho..?

My first day in Class VIII. There is a very pleasant surprise and a dreadful news as well awaiting me in the new session

Mr. Lucius Gabriel is no more our Math's teacher. A delightful gift in the new academic year

And the real bad news, Joyce changed his school. Got transferred to the famous top English medium school in the same town. Inarguably, this school produces brilliant Matriculates every year

The news of his departure saddens me, for he has been my closest buddy and confidante from Class V. Am going to miss him terribly. What a bad news. Am rattled!

Vibha comes to school during second session. She didn't want to miss her very first day in High school, she claims. It's a bad omen, she adds up. Not quite sure, but I think, Lakshmi aunt might've pushed her to come. Otherwise, this lazy lady, Ms. Dwarf rolls back and enjoys being at home

'Trrrinnnngg..', goes the long bell. Day comes to close

Am waiting for Vibha under the jackfruit tree right in front of my class

On our way back home, she looks into my eyes and then, instantaneously drops a bomb

Her father, Appu uncle has this idea of relocating to city, near to our school. Her older sister Raji and brother Bharath also study in our school. But they both have their own compatriots from house to school and back. We all four never make it together to our school

'Amma is not in agreement. Also, me, Raji, Bharath, no one is happy with this plan', she said

We all know, Appu uncle is stubborn and hard-hearted. He is nothing like my Appa

'Why are you shifting from here'? I can't control my anxiety

My mind boils. What if they shift out from my neighbourhood?

'No idea Sanju'. Appa says, 'it will be easier for him to make it to the shop', Vibha

Appu uncle's upholstery shop sits in the middle of a busy junction in the main city

But what if he commutes from the present location? What's wrong with this Appu uncle?

Am restless. All those who are closer to my chest are quitting my life one by one leaving me behind all alone lurching around in the wilderness!

Granny's unwell lately. Not talkative as she used to be once

What if Vibha too leaves?

'Sanju, what are you thinking'? Vibha

'Nothing', my voice shows no life

I try hard masking what's going on in my mind. I must conceal my tears, or else, she will think am chicken hearted

She knows am timid..ignobly timid

Vibha looks at me. She rotates her eyeballs. Smiles at me with her lower lip clinching with her tooth

'C'mon, cheer up Sanju. Be cheerful man. Don't be moody. I don't want to see you like this', Vibha

'Am fearful Vibha, can't be cheerful after you broke this ill news', I want to shout out the words to Vibha, but can't..am tight lipped..

'Don't be so easily expressive', I console my heart

We stroll together. I copy her style of walk of late. Slow and lazy with a snail's pace. Nevertheless, her steps look attractive, short and crispy

'Sanju, when you walk, your knees are not bending. It's not natural', our sports trainer pointed out once

'You want me to correct my gait', huh? I ask expecting a remedial action

'As long as it's not leading to any deformity, it's kay Sanju', quipped the over-sized physical trainer

While nearing her house, Vibha gives a naughty look and chuckles, and then she runs inside at one fell swoop

I feel something fishy with her unfamiliar expression

'You Ms. Dwarf', I chase her down and catch hold of her mane

'Ouch! Leave me, you brat', Vibha screams

She turns around and smacks my other wrist with a toy cricket bat. It's a mangled plastic bat

'What's happening kids', Lakshmi aunt kicks in

She looks being bothered by Vibha's scream

'Are you shifting out from here aunt? I suddenly ask

'Shifting? Where? Disbelief on her face. Mix of surprise and dismay

'This bloody Ms. Dwarf told me', am furious

'She played a prank with you Sanju. Take it easy', Lakshmi aunt

'Will see you Ms. Dwarf', I glare at Vibha before leaving

Oh My God! My heart was pumping hard all these while. Felt like, my heart skipped a beat

Can't think of leaving out Vibha a single day. Granny and Vibha remain my biggest weakness. My Achilles heel!

Either of them departs, I seriously doubt whether I will survive those moments. I will be soulless if such a thing happens

Day by day, life's becoming a high-wire performance. Sometimes, life plays cruel jokes

How will I overcome my fears? Unsure and vulnerable about the next moment

I am scared of dark, being alone, strange sturdy men, Mr. Lucius Gabriel, Amma, Nakul bhaiya, and monsters and all those scary imaginary creatures. Am also afraid when it's dark and stormy. As I grow old, I may be able to conquer these fears and outgrow them..

Will I or will I not?

Chapter 14

Finally, the Big day arrives. Today is the biggest festival. On this day, I've blanket permission from Amma for flying kite with my friends, subject to her terms and conditions. I agree with the same, unconditionally..

A fortnight before festivals, me and Somi charter our program for the day. Program starts from keeping awake the whole night of festival eve and ends with festival day supper. We had fixed some indoor games on the previous day night, bathe in the wee hours, and a visit to the Narsimhamurthi temple. Come back and have breakfast, and I will be then, off with friends till lunch time. It's going to be real fun this time around. I've been longing for this day quite a lot

Somi too has some plan of action with Baby, Uma aunt, and Radha chachi. Amma joins them sometimes. But, I never see Amma in a lighter mood playing games with neighbourhood women. And when she does, it's like Eid ka Chand!

This big festival is celebrated by One and All. Religion or community never poses a challenge

Another popular entertainment during this time is the tradition of Swing, which is known as Oonjal in regional term. This is another great fun. Traditionally, the festival stretches to 10 days, and the Tenth day is the mega festival. During these 10 days leading to the mega festival, which is the carnival event, a swing is slung on a high branch of a tree and normally decorated with any variety of Yellow flowers

But, my biggest infatuation is kite. Whenever I see kites flying in the sky, the very scene refreshes my mind and brings me off the shelf happiness. I keep looking at the slowly rising kite reaching higher and higher. When I watch the dancing kite up in the sky, I feel a great sense of ambition. I simply get lost from the sheer exuberance I feel while watching the colourfully decorated kites dangling with variety of colours and different shapes. Wow! It's feast to my eyes!

It is an art to take the kite to dizzy heights in the sky. Many of my friends are not conversant with this technique. It is not simple, as a matter of fact. One needs to wait for a strong wind to blow, with your assistant holding your kite up by the bridle point in accurate position. If there is sufficient wind, the assistant alerts the captain who pulls the string, and he simultaneously releases the kite. This is exactly the time when the captain runs with the thread roll releasing it concurrently. This pulling force will let your kite go right up. If the kite flies away from you a little, then you can pull it towards the line so that the kite climbs vertically up

If the wind is not conducive or playing tricky, the smart assistant should not release the kite, and will notify the captain to wait patiently

A good assistant reads the direction of the wind correctly and contributes effectively towards the ultimate cause. The kite, which reaches the highest in the sky, and lands back safe unscathed after 2 or 3 hours of flying wins the first prize. This may be a roll of twine, 2 sketch pens, or a quarter dozen fancy pencils fitted with eraser at the bottom!

Atchu is my regular assistant. He is reliable. His sense of reading wind strength and direction is great. More importantly, he knows exactly how my mind works

He knows very well that I do not compromise on my assistant's technical capabilities. He is proud to be my deputy, and doesn't like to leave the slot open for anyone else to come and occupy

But this time, I think to give chance to Vishnu, just for a change, but Atchu wouldn't be much pleased with this

It's a real entertainer if there are four or five captains fly their kites together. The person who cuts the opponent's tail wins bonus points. Without tail, the kites starts spinning in the sky and eventually will comes down or get dropped on the top of a huge tree or a hill. In multiple kite contests, the person with the last kite in the air is the ultimate winner

The day opens up with a wholesome breakfast. This is has to be resplendent, to say the least. Amma ensures our festive breakfast is always unique, and not the ordinary Idly, Dosa type which is cooked in our neighbourhood. This is followed by a grand vegetarian feast. Truly in line with the festival tradition. Amma never compromises on quality of food cooked in her kitchen

She takes it as a prestige issue every year. This area is her pride

Palappam with thick coconut milk is the breakfast today. My all-time favourite. I gobble it up till the belly hits my nose tip. I counted till four and then loses count. Stomach swells to the fullest!

I'm restless since morning. Raring to go. I can't afford to be late to go to grounds

'What are you dreaming about, huh'? Granny's voice

I look at her face with no expression. I await a final nod from Amma

'I see your friends Ramesh, Udhay, and Sunil leave with their kites', Granny's Intelligence inputs

I know, her inputs are reliable. No need to cross check

I go inside the kitchen. I find Amma and Somi cutting vegetables

Somi can't even hold the knife properly, she is acting like a professional chef to impress Amma

Appa had breakfast and left home. He will come back after a stroll

Nakul bhaiya suddenly storms inside. He has not had breakfast, if I'm not wrong

Now, what's he up to.. I make a quick analysis. He doesn't look to be in festive mood

'Give me 5 rupees', Nakul bhaiya to Amma

'What, 5 rupees'? Amma's eyes pop out of the sockets. 'I don't have', Amma

I am surprised. Did I hear it right?

This is least expected from Amma. I never see Amma refuse him pittance. Nakul bhaiya demands money or other consents, Amma makes it a point that she never disappoints him

'I want 5 rupees right now. My friends are going for movie. I can't miss it', Nakul bhaiya

'I don't have. Take from Appa, let him come. I remember, last time, you went for a movie and fought with the man at the ticket counter', Amma

'I can't give you money. Stay here and enjoy the festival delicacies. I've prepared mouth-watering dishes. It's a real gem to be at home today', Amma pleads

'Come Nakul, eat breakfast before you go out', Granny asks him

Nakul bhaiya loses his cool. Suddenly goes berserk, and throws tantrums all over. Kicking vessels and starts screaming

Shows resentment to Granny as well

He'll screw up everything today. I smell a rat. Nakul bhaiya is in a disruptive mood

On such a day, he can play the spoilsport. He had staged similar violent stuff in the past, especially on festival days

He can't take 'No' for an answer

It is futile trying to pacify him. One can't reason with him. Even Appa can't

Amma throws the knife down and gets up. She too loses her cool

Scarcely, they lock horns, and what follows are horrifying scenes

'Amma..' Amma calls out to Granny. Granny is Amma's last resort on such intricate situations

Granny bails out Amma using her command and clout as the senior most citizen of the family. But not sure this time, Granny's power play will work out. Things are not looking conducive at the moment

'Come, have breakfast Nakul', Amma pleads trying to control her anger

Amma is trying really hard to make both ends meet with Appa's meagre income from our small petty sales setup. We had our own big business shop in another town. But my younger sibling Moli's prolonged illnesses and her ultimate demise consumed all our richness. Yet, she didn't survive

When we fall from grace, the impact is too tough to handle. We are going through the same harsh repercussions. Amma is at a loss to come to terms with that. May be, Nakul bhaiya too!

Nakul bhaiya throws out his festival breakfast and flounces out. He pushes me to side from his way

It's now almost certain, Amma is not going to allow me for kite flying. She looks desperate and furious at Nakul bhaiya's unprecedented behaviour

Overall, am a victim of circumstances today. My small little dreams never take wings and fly high, like my beautiful kite. I had invested two days and a good Three rupees to make it real. All in vain. I dreamed of making this festival memorable. Yes, it has become a real memorable one for years to come!

Granny reads my mind

Looking at her sunken darkened eyes, I nod my head crossword. I read the helplessness in her eyes

Heartbroken, I sit in a corner on the bare floor. Looking at myself futile and worthless

Unlike Appa, Nakul bhaiya isn't cool headed. Had he been so, our lives as a whole ought to have been pleasantly different. He has become a perfectly spoiled brat!

He is Amma's dearest. Amma cooks for him special dishes, takes special care of his clothing, toils around for him, and above all, grants small allowances. To her, Nakul bhaiya isn't less than any hero straight from a movie screen

But Nakul bhaiya, doesn't reciprocate the same way

On the contrary, Amma means everything for me. Sadly, she never realizes that. Even when she would ask me to clean the whole house, I wouldn't say no to her. I can move mountains to win her heart. That is the truth!

But Nakul bhaiya is just the opposite. He would ignore her advice however worth it is. Yet, without her own conscience, she has spoiled him with her over indulgence. He gets what he wants without actually having to do anything to get it. Even without being an obedient son!

He relies on Amma for anything. When Amma gets sick or goes to visit her relatives to a distant place, Nakul bhaiya undergoes a hard time. He would argue with Granny without any purpose just out of frustration of not having Amma around

May be, he too loves Amma. But unable to exhibit. Who knows, he loves me too!

Through the partially dismantled window, half of which is sent for repair, I see the gloomy face of Suresh. Atchu and Vishnu are also there. Impatience reflects on all 3 faces. A thick coat of disappointment overshadowing the impatience on their faces

Amma suspends cooking, looks silent. On such troubled times, her silence is deafening. Whenever she keeps prolonged silence, it is a bad sign. We all know that

Somi hasn't retired. Seems to be still active in kitchen. During such grim circumstances, she keeps the momentum going. Calling out from kitchen without any specific purpose or asking assistance which would be not necessary at that moment, and stuffs like that..

Somi, at times is very witty. She cracks classic jokes when the whole house is in a tense mood. Her jokes are a cut above. But, one takes a little time to conceive it. Next level jokes..

She's the one who can galvanise the mood of entire family when the chips are down. Borrowing a modern commentator's language, I can say, Somi is a 'game changer'

Appa's not yet back. He had had breakfast before leaving

I see Suresh display Kathakali Mudras, with such perfection that even a veteran artist in the field would be proud. He's asking me to come out. He's an expert in communication techniques using Mudras

He should be better off in the field of Doordarshan News for Hearing Impaired!

'Please leave now. I can't come Suresh'. I display my head out through the window and inform them in a dampen voice

'We all have been waiting only for you Sanju. It's very bad', chorus from Atchu and Vishnu

'If I come, it would be even worse', I say sarcastically. 'If Amma happens to see you all, then had it', I caution them trying hard to sweep my grief under the carpet

After all, it's not new to me

My dreams have always been small but closest to my heart. But suddenly, it shatters into small fragments, like the old story of The Milkmaid and her Pail, leaving me devastated!

'Kay Sanju. Let's catch up in the evening. I'll bring payasam for all', Suresh

'Let's hope Suresh'. I show him Thumbs Up and softly shut the window

No kite flying. No delightful moments. My long-awaited festivities have gone with the wind!

The long-awaited festival day finally comes to a painful abrupt end. Our festive lunch is inconclusive, so is the supper

It's bedtime. Granny rolls up her tiny frame inside her favourite Black military blanket. This was gifted to her by a grand son working in Army. This blanket is as rough as Sandpaper, and I wonder how could Granny spent the whole night inside this horrendous sleeping kit peacefully like a child!

Am inside an over-sized woolly pullover, caught in the wilderness of my bitter solitude!

Chapter 15

Don't know. Thoughts are disintegrated and scattered around. Back from school very late. Nobody is seen outside house

Radha chachi comes in. She's Uma aunt's younger sister. Stout and Black with not-so-pleasant physical features. Corpulent looking. She's Amma's most reliable neighbour and trusted confidante

'She looks rough, but has a very sweet heart. I trust her. Just the opposite of Uma', Amma would say frequently

'Where're all chachi'? I ask

'Sulo Didi had a fall in the afternoon. In hospital', Radha chachi

'What happened to Amma', am at the brink of a cry

'No details Sanju. Come, I will take you. It's District Government Hospital', she says

I rush inside; throw my books into the wooden box. This box is my very private property. Equipped with a small pad lock and a tiny half-inch key, the same I hide from Somi. She is inquisitive, and hardly gives me any space. Her prying eyes follow me day in, day out

Poor Granny is all alone. Sitting in a round chair, almost drifting out of the frame. She looks weary. I grab her hands and kiss her left cheek. It's warm and moist. She embraces me with her weak arms. I could feel tremors in her arms. Tremors of weakness. Tremors of helplessness. Tremors of haplessness. I can't take it anymore. Her eyes fill when she looks at me

'Careful Granny. Am back in a short while. Will bring you food from the restaurant, your favourite meal with fish curry. Don't worry, kay'? I say

Granny gives a pale smile in return

I ensure my small coins are safe in my Khaki uniform trunks' pockets

Suddenly a wild thought pulls me back from the door

What if something happens to Granny? She is all alone back home. Who'll take care of her in case of an urgency? She is extremely debilitated. What if she tries to get up and her weak legs give up?

Somi is in the Hosp with Amma. Probably, Appa will make it directly from the shop at night

But who is with Granny? She looks traumatized. I shouldn't, rather, I can't afford to leave her in this biting loneliness

I come out. Radha chachi awaits me outside

'Chachi, you may leave. Am not coming. Here's no one with Granny. Must cook food for her', I said

'Don't you want to see Amma'? Her eyes come out riddled with a big question mark

'I'll visit her tomorrow morning, on the way to school', I said

'Kay then Sanju. I'll go and pay a visit. Will update you once am back', Radha chachi leaves

I get back. Move to kitchen

'Will make hot filter coffee now, Granny. Am not going anywhere leaving you', my pitch was high enough so that Granny hears it

'Good my child', Granny promptly responds from the room. Her voice tells it all. She is relieved

I must take a small recess to wash my face and change over to domestic clothing. I slip out to the rear side of the house in a hush

I take a sauce pan and fill it with two-and-a cups of water. Granny may take some extra sips

Successfully lighted the kerosene stove after 3 failed attempts

Bring it to boil. Add 2 heaped spoons of filter coffee. Close the pan with an Aluminium lid. Let it settle for a while

After a couple of minutes, I carefully transfer the coffee to mugs and come to Granny

'Hello Granny, here's the coffee for you, with love from your Sanju beta'. I notice the broad smile on her face

Hands the bigger cup to Granny

While sipping the hot coffee, 'what happened to Amma'? I delicately ask Granny

'Nakul is missing since morning today. Somi went to wake him up, he was missing from the bed', Granny

Am shell shocked! Nakul bhaiya is absconding..? Where has he gone?

Now, I realize why was Granny looking so frightened and nervous when I came from school

'Sulo checked with his friends. Went all around the neighbourhood and visited all his possible hangouts. Couldn't find him. She was frustrated, and by 4 in the afternoon, she had a bout of severe headache and she fainted', Granny goes on

Why has Nakul bhaiya done it? Am unaware of many things happen in the family right under my nose

'Somi was here, right'? I ask

'Yes, she alerted Radha and Uma. Uma called an auto rickshaw. Somi accompanied Sulo to Hosp while Uma had a domestic emergency and couldn't go. Radha too stayed back. She couldn't go', Granny explains in detail

'Shall I get something for dinner Granny, before it's too late'? I ask

'Let's wait for Radha. Amma might ensure our dinner. She will arrange to send it across', Granny

'May be you're right'. But am not very hopeful

How could she arrange supper for us when she is in Hosp bed? Granny has gone nuts!

Must finish my homework. Some tough comprehension work in English and an essay preparation on Social Reformation from Social Studies. While I conveniently forego Mathematics

Regional language poem recital competition is coming up. Am considered a strong contender by Mr. Balram, our regional language teacher

Last time, I recited a poem written by a renowned poet in a different rhyme, tuned by me instantly. It was a sudden burst of fun with my moods. My fancy style goes well with the lyrics. Whole Class claps

However, Maths remains a tough nut cut to crack. I don't want to crack it either! Hell with Maths. I don't care a heck. It's become my nemesis. I wouldn't be able to it. Never!

Amma can't bear a scratch happen to Nakul bhaiya. He is her Ladla beta. Amma is not going to be normal till she sees his face again. It's going to be a test by fire for Appa too. Amma wouldn't spare Appa. She is going to hold Appa responsible for the whole chaos happening around. Appa is Amma's soft target almost always. Once again, hard times await poor Appa. No options. He is totally disadvantaged!

It's about half past 8. Someone knocks the door. I come out. Granny takes a light doze. Not wanting to disturb her

It's Radha chachi at the door

'Hello Radha chachi', I greet her

'Sanju, take this'. She hands me a polythene bag

'Amma asked me to buy food for you. Rice and fish curry. Luckily Hob-Nob was open', Radha chachi

Hob-Nob is a newly opened restaurant at Kanjikuzhy town. We get tasty modern cuisines here. One will find modern fancy amenities here. Run by twin brothers. Sons of another well-to-do shopkeeper in the town. Some dishes we get here are only heard of, but lip smacking once tasted

'How about Amma? Is she kay'? I ask

'Spoke to her. Would come home in the morning. She had retired to bed when I left. She had asked you to be taking care of yourself and Granny at night', Radha chachi

'Kay, thanks chachi' I say

She walks down to her house. It's just a stone's throw from my house, but slightly up sloping pathway

Granny silently eats supper

After dinner, Granny hits the sack straight

Am too tired. Try hard to sleep. But something strange from the subconscious mind pulls me back from the present. It constantly flings me to the hostility of wild thoughts

Where's Nakul bhaiya?

Where has he gone?

Has he had eaten food?

Where's he sheltering now?

Too many questions hover around. Mind is occupied with a myriad of feelings and emotions mangled up to one another. Horrible mix of irrational thoughts..

Am I falling prey to emotional dissonance?

Unable to rationalise. Unable to find solace

But there's certainly one thing. Am a huge disappointment everywhere

I dip my face on to the pillow as if trying to dig deep inside and hide my face from the world

'Sanju', Granny's sweet voice scented with betel nuts wakes me up

'Oops! It's past eight', I spring up from the bedding and run out

Radha chachi brings Black coffee. Steamy hot. Seems straight from the stove

Our house is in a populated area, mostly, infested with humble dwellings sans a few big shots living very close. Neighbours are generally into small-time businesses, some run petty shops spinning marginal revenue sufficient enough to take care of family needs and children's education

Radha chachi helps Amma. Her husband Nattu chacha doesn't possess polished societal etiquettes, but not a harmful being

'Come Sanju, drink coffee. You like it, right'? Radha chachi calls

'Nattu chacha came too late at night. Nakul seems to have run away. He was seen loitering in the Railway Station premises. Nattu chacha's friend saw him there in the morning about 6, but he didn't feel anything suspicious', Radha chachi

'Kay chachi. Thanks for the coffee', I withdraw from the scene. It's already late for school

Am unusually late today. I get ready for school. Not feeling charged up. This is quite uncharacteristic of me on a school day morning. It's 20 past 9 and am still at home!

I causally give a glance down at the frontage tarred road. It's in the vicinity of hardly 100 meters. I see Amma and Somi alighting from an auto rickshaw

Somi carries a small travel bag containing their clothes

'Granny, Amma has come', I run to the road

'Amma', I call and go near, holding her hand, but she shrugs it off

'Don't touch', Amma's bland voice

Amma doesn't smile. Her face looks grim. I want to speak to her, but she wouldn't. She walks normal, but lacks strength

Somi watchfully fetches her home and makes her sit in an armed chair. Amma doesn't look at Granny too, who seems to be puzzled at Amma's strange behaviour

'Why are you here? Go to school. Somi is here for my assistance. Clear off'. Amma's harsh words pointing to me

'Yes Amma, I was about to leave for school when I saw you come. Thought to greet you and then leave'

'Hum', she makes a solid sound

Can't distinguish. Am extremely perturbed at her bizarre attitude

I kiss Granny's skeleton cheek and give her a pampering handshake. She smiles with her upper and lower lips furrowed inward making ultra modern art form of wrinkles on her face. I slowly step out for school. Vibha must have left long ago

My feet are not moving. Am drastically lost once again! Why is Amma so toxic to me?

Amma's actions and words frequently hurt me. She nullifies my accomplishments. She never congratulates me about the marks I score in English or any of my good deeds. Not even once, she appreciated my domestic help at home. And on the other hand, she picks me for everything I do. Control me in every department of life. I am done!

Somi follows me to the tarred road without getting noticed by Amma

'Sanju, Appa came to Hosp last night. Amma asked him to leave immediately and find the whereabouts of Nakul bhaiya'

She warned Appa, 'I don't want to see you again without my son'

'Anything you know, why Nakul bhaiya did flee home'? I can't lock up this question inside me any further

Somi comes further close, almost dipping her broad round face inside my right ear. She literally pokes her lips into my ear. Her warm breath is felt inside my Eustachian tube

'Don't tell anyone Sanju. Appa received some serious complaints about Nakul bhaiya from some of his reliable friends. He has become more unruly after leaving school' right'? Somi

'Yes, we all know that', I replied

Somi's eyes take a complete 360 degree like that of a frog watching Amma's movements. Her eyes are as clever as a Hawk's. Who knows it better?

Her probing eyes stick on my face again finally..

It's her nature. Though nobody's watching, she pretends being watched by people around and tends to be carefully discreet

Am impatient, 'Ya, tell me for God sake. Am damn late for school'

'That festivaly day night, Appa looked quite disturbed and nervous. He gave a nice dressing-down to Nakul bhaiya for spoiling his life and bringing bad name to the family', Somi

'Kay, what next'?

'Nakul bhaiya uses bandy words, and Appa gives a tight slap. Seeing this Amma comes running and pushes Appa aside, and pulled Nakul bhaiya inside. Poor Appa leaves the scene without a word'

'Nakul bhaiya was enraged. Sanju, I think, this could be the reason'

'By the way, where's Appa now'? I want to know

'Yesterday night, Appa caught a Redeye bus as there was no train, and left for Amma's native place. He might drop in at some of our relatives, Somi sums it up

'Bye Sanju', Somi runs back home. Somi's happy having a ball at home being excused by Amma from attending school

Somi seldom discloses family secrets to me, and when she does, it is with too many conditions

This seems an exception

Two days pass, dull and uneventful

Amma scarcely speaks or eats. Her face looks scary. Very scary

She doesn't come out. 'Sulo can't lock her eyes with neighbourhood', Granny says

Eventually, we receive news about Nakul bhaiya. He's with my cousin brother's wife's house. They grew doubt on Nakul bhaiya's sudden arrival, but don't ask him any intriguing questions, for they all like Nakul bhaiya very much

They wisely send a wire to Appa giving brief details

'Please send him back today itself. Sulo hasn't had proper food and sleep ever since he left', Appa sends a return wire requesting Nakul bhaiya's return journey details

On the Third day, we see Appa and Nakul bhaiya come together to home. It's a dark, dull late evening. Appa escorts him from the Railway station

Amma is sitting at the doorstep, anxiously waiting to see Nakul bhaiya

Seeing them, Amma jumps up in joy, suddenly breaks into tears

'Here's your son. I've brought him back', Appa is visibly filled with emotion. His words sound wet

He spontaneously turns back and walks away to aimlessly...

Amma doesn't bother to care. Her son is back and that's it!

Rush of fresh blood into her veins. She suddenly looks healthy and robust. She finds new spirit and happiness, comes near to Nakul bhaiya. He looks down to the floor like a culprit

'Oh my son', Amma hugs Nakul bhaiya and slaps him frantically over and over. It's Amma's disguised show of exuberant love and affection. Strong expression of endearment

Somewhere in the corner of my inner self, those moments sow the seeds of extreme jealous about Nakul bhaiya

Appa never slapped him again if memory leads me right. Let alone that, Appa hasn't had a purposeful discussion with him on any anything. Never again. With Amma in front like a Senapati, Nakul bhaiya looks emotionally formidable!

He is her real son. Am just optional. Like a loose screw. Pick it and fix or throw it, if doesn't fit!

Chapter 16

A few months later

Academic year's in progress

My Class VIII final exams are around the corner. I've finally come to terms with the fancy language left behind by the Britons. Gave up long ago on Maths and Physics much to my own delight. Still try to tame Physics though it's not that exciting, but when Physics gets mixed with the applicability of formulae, I hate it too. It's just like Maths in another form. No much difference. It really bugs!

It's a huge blessing that Mr. Lucius Gabriel is not our Maths teacher. May be, he is not qualified enough to handle high school students. One Ms. Sleeba Kurien takes over his place in our class. She's tall, fair, and pretty. A pious woman with true virtues who is extremely noble in her profession. She speaks excellent English, but with a typical regional accent. She's a crowd puller!

Not sure whether her language has a considerable percentage of mother tongue influence. The whole Class is present during her class without a single student being absent. We lean forward on the desk, rest our cheek on the biceps, and leisurely see and listen to her Mathematical diagrams, Trigonometry, cross multiplications et al. Her command over the students is too good. Anyways, am never able to accept the fundamental concept of having to prove why a square is a square!

Quite often, am unable to relish her class merely due to the fact that despite all her style and charm, after all, she is teaching Maths, which I've extreme and intense animosity with, and my antagonistic conflict with the subject refuses to go away!

Other than me, there are a few 'Maths Haters 'too in the class. But am the most hardcore among all. Standing tall scoring consistently in reverse order in tests at all levels

However, Ms. Sleeba Kurien once upon a time, was impressed by my attitude and behaviour only until I scored 13 out of 50in Christmas exams, keeping my record of failures proud and intact!

She never again smiles at me, is another case of rubbing salt to my wounded ego, which I always mimicked to have, but never really possessed!

In plain language, I try my level best to embrace Maths with open arms. By the virtue of having an excellent teacher, I know it's now or never. But I fall flat never to rise again whenever I bump into equations, fractions, cross multiplications, and above all, Trigonometry. It's a real hell!

I never get excited about numbers and formulae to the level am, comparable with language or other subjects that are easier for me to personally connect with

It's of course, my very personal opinion that I dare say, Maths as abstract and irrelevant, highly esoteric

Maths tends to generate strong negative traits in me even now. I strongly feel, if Ms. Sleeba Kurien had taught me from Class V, she could have transformed me in toto. Nevertheless, you can't change a beginning all over again!

Not long ago, I've cut short on my fantasy thoughts. It doesn't enthral me any more like once it used to be. Given the course of action my life takes me through, I consider myself socially anxious. Unable to curb my wild bewildering emotions. Domestic insecurity creepin. Finding myself aloof from my peer group. A self-imposed isolation in a nutshell. I ardently wish at times, I had not been born!

It's the beginning of Summer. Days are warmer and longer. Nights are very short. Hit the sack and close your eyes, it's next morning

One Sunday afternoon, 3 or half past 3. It's the hottest time of the day in India

Suddenly, Vibha drops in

Wow! It's the rarest of a rare occasion, like the appearance of Halley's Comet

'What a delightful shock'! I exclaim. Vibha or her sister Raji barely pays visit to our house

'I've come to Savitri aunt' Vibha whispered while discreetly throwing a look at Amma with the corner of her eyes

Savitri aunt's another neighbor of ours. She operates a part-time grocery shop from her house. But only selective goods like jaggery, sugar, dry fish, coconut, onion, green chillies, or turmeric. One may not find all these listed items available together. Sometimes, jaggery and dry fish or some other times, sugar and onion can be obtained from thiscommercial-cum-domestic outlet. I bet, one can't get a condiment here when it's most urgently needed. Say, if the curry is boiling and you at once need some spice or green chilli, you run to her, it's almost sure and certain that you're not going to get it there. Above all, there's a thumb rule; the shop works only when it suits her. If she's busy domestically, either you wait at the door step till she finishes her work or better make a second visit later. So, the fact of the matter is, Savitri aunt's doing a hanky-panky business, which in any way is not beneficial to both parties!

It's been noticed many times, Vibha's not very comfortable dealing with my Amma

Amma's not looking happy either seeing Vibha with me close by

'I've come to see you Sanju. You're not seen of late. Designedly avoiding me, I think', Vibha, keeps her voice as low as she can

'Nothing of that sort Vibha', I guide her outside from Amma's detective eyes. She looks inquisitive

I look into the bottom of her eyes. She has a pair of fairly good round eyes. Glowing cheeks reflects the afternoon sunrays passing across our open-air veranda, now partially damaged, and looks like the remains straight from the site of an ancient fort dates back to B.C.

She is in a midi skirt and round-neck top hanging loose. Her stilettos footwear enhances her height by a good 2 inches, but still short of average height of girls in her age

She doesn't speak much. Her eyes look sheepish but vividly excited. Mix of both. I can't define

what's written all over her face. But overwhelmingly enthralled am at the moment!

She springs up suddenly, as if she smells a naughty rat sneak out of me

'Let me leave Sanju. Don't forget to take me to school tomorrow morning', Vibha leaves

It's close to 4 in the afternoon. I run to the field with all my courage defying Amma's inflexible list of Do's and Don'ts. My heart is filled with sparkling joy. It has been found precisely a little while ago..

My heart's humming the evergreen verses from the great poet,

'A host, of Golden Daffodils

Beside the lake, beneath the trees,

Fluttering and dancing in the breeze'

Ramesh, Udhay, Atchu, Vishnu, Suresh..I can see all of them in the field from a distance

'Hello Sanju', Suresh greets me clasping my fingers. 'It's been long since we met like this', his words enclosed in despondence

'Hello', I hit him lovingly on his back

'Come Suresh. Today's another one-to-one fight with me and Ramesh. I've something to prove to him', am excited. Raring to go with another game Vs Ramesh. I can wrestle an alligator now!

Ramesh bombarded me in the last encounter; can't forget that easy. He shot me down in less than 1 hour. I'm seeking revenge today

'Come Sanju, let's fight it out', Ramesh comes close. He looks solid. His words sound like an open challenge to my ego

'Am going to kill you man, today'. I affirm to myself

Atchu marks border lines horizontally at both ends, and claps to alert me and Ramesh

'Sanju and Ramesh, on your spots. No time to waste', Atchu shouts from the other end

Atchu looks excited. He can't wait any more to see the big fight coming up. Obviously, we two are the best ones in the native ball games in our category. If we join together as a team, none of the boys from our locality can floor us

Here we go. Match starts. Ramesh, as usual, looks cool and composed. Characteristics of a great player

Whereas, I flip my lid more often than not in a catch-22 position. Very vibrant

Atchu spins the coin. I call Heads

I win the toss. Am going to serve. Luck favors me this time

When I win the toss, I always serve first. Making the first move gives me advantage

'Yes, Ramesh, take this', here I roll the ball in the air and bang with my right arm from the hip level

'This is with love from me Sanju', Ramesh kicks it back with his right forefoot curving downward

'Oops', I sniff

His service return is too good. No problem. It's my strength too

When 2 players with similar characteristics, having same strengths and vulnerabilities are in combat mode, the outcome is a great match for the spectators. A great gala match. When me and Ramesh are at loggerheads, this is what our friends get to watch

Match moves to the next level. Our trunks and summer vests drench in sweat. Our naked feet ache, and I hurt my right foot hitting a loose stone

I look at Ramesh. He looks rock-hard. Am wearing down

But I'll smash him today. I've a promise to accomplish

'Up..up..up..up', friends clap echoing. Cheering both, for they know, it's a clash of titans and they don't want to see the climax so soon

Solid 1 hour elapses. The match is tantalizingly poised with me having advantage. I might win the match with a couple of good returns and winners

Here happens the most unexpected. The one last thing we wanted, rather I wanted

Amma hastily walks up to the middle as if caught in the storm. She has a bludgeon in her right hand

Friends give me timely alert. I look at the weapon in her hand. It's strong enough to smash the head of a buffalo. Looks like the handle of an axe

Amma storms at me and before I take an evading action, she swings it in the air and bashes it down my right knee!

'Ouch', I cried aloud. The pain is unbearable

'Please don't' Atchu and Suresh jump into the middle, but they're too late

'Go away', Amma pushes them aside. She looks hysteric

While am wriggling in the dust, she simply walks away ordering me to get back, causing tremors on the earth. She doesn't look back even once!

Atchu and Vishnu help me stand in one leg. Ramesh supports my trunks to be in place. I literally crawl back home. I don't have the lungs to look at my friends' face as Amma causes irreparable damage to my self-respect. It's a huge humiliation. I no more have any dignity. Am tormented. Brutally crushed to mere dust. Am huffing and puffing..unable to breathe enough Oxygen!

Thank God. No fracture. But my right tibia is excruciatingly painful. Unable to move an inch. Impact area is puffy and swollen up with Blackish-Blue contusion

Night, I said No to supper, as a mark of protest. I writhe in pain. Oh My God, am unable to contain the agony of my heart. It violently pounds as if in the midst of a battle field!

Appa comes and sees me; utters something to Amma. She replies something hard and Appa's voice sinks in

Poor Granny is giving me warm water sponge

'You sleep Granny', I mumble

'No my child. I can't see you in this misery. I must die before I see you struggle at her hands once again', Granny's voice disrupts

I take the kerosene lamp and turn to her face

Am shocked! It's a bone-chilling feel down my spine. Tears roll down my Granny's grey face. Her pale eyes bear no more life. Tear drops stick on her cheeks; partially glow in dim light, but no graphic reflections. Am deeply moved. Her hapless poster brings tears into my eyes. Granny looks really pathetic, and the pain it gives is more than my own!

The meek Matriarch of the family! I embrace her tight, for she is my last refuge

After long efforts, I put her to sleep

This pain is killing me. Makes me crazy

I slowly open my note book. In the flickering light, I go through my last week's English homework, which won me the top score in the class

'My Mother'

'My Mother's tall and fair complexioned. She does so many things to keep our family happy, without expecting anything in return. Appa buys her a new sari on a festival day. This makes her happy and her face blossoms like a flower. She's like a best friend as she takes care of everything we need. My mother's the synonym of love and kindness. As a whole, Mother's very presence on the earth provides happiness to the enduring human race. Her smiling face removes all my sorrows and stress and makes me elated. It's simply a truth that there's no one other like a Mother'

I've my foot in my mouth! I can't believe my own words about what I wrote about my Amma...

May be, not everyone likes you, but there are some very special people in our lives that are considered exceptions. In my case, it's my Granny. However, I always assume that mothers are members of a close circle of loved people whom we cherish in our regular interactions. Sadly, this's not the case with me

I've 2 choices here. Either I battle it out or have an ugly and pitiful death like a worm. I must take the first option

I must resurrect like the Greek mythical bird. The symbol of Immortality!

Am pushed to extreme. This is a dead end. My life must take a carefully crafted U-turn from this intersection. This night is going to transform me. A violent, phenomenal metamorphosis is bound to happen in me

From a frangible adolescent boy to a stubborn, brave-hearted, strong-fisted man I must become

From now on, I can only hope. Let anyone walk away from your life, hope is the one thing that still remains with you. Hope is not mesmerizing. It's not magical thinking. Hope is a smooth slice of emotion, a state of mind, motivation, that despite setbacks and obstacles, despite hardships and misfortunes, despite the unknown last part of your own story, you believe that your life will work for the better. There's certainly something else beyond this ruthless world!

Does the legacy of an unkind and insensitive mother babble over into a boy's psyche and his ability to connect to the opposite sex in methods and resources that are distinctive?

What will happen to me as a full-blown young man whose understanding of a woman is shaped by the first woman he encountered — a detached or hypercritical mother?

Can't control my tears. I start to snivel. Am decimated to Zero and thrown under a fast fleeing bus!

I must fight my apprehensions. Structure new perceptions and interpretations to find a new me!

I submerge my wet teary face into the pages of my note. What a piece of crap! 'My Mother'!

Chapter 17

Time swifts past. A not-so eventful Class IX passes through. We have almost all the same faculty in Matric too

Eventually, when Am here at the land mark turning point in the life of a student who is an Indian student in India, I start making my presence felt in exams, more or less..in Science group and English, the one tongue, which most of our countrymen are having a crush with!

In a few weeks from now, our Matric exams are slated to begin. Almost all of us have been together from Class V

Our uniform had changed from high school, all boys with White shirt and either single Dhoti or Double Dhoti compatible with our height to avoid any conflict in appearance and dress code of our institution. Girls, long Raising Blue colour skirt and white shirt

However, I insist for double Dhoti at home though I don't figure among tallest pupils in the class. Since am constantly giving restless Dhoti moments to Amma, finally, she gets me 2 Double Dhotis. But now the real problem starts. It's oversized and doesn't fit my skewer-like frame. With great support from Nakul bhaiya, I manage to tie it in my hip and then fold it upward from the knee level. But again, it opens and slips down frequently due to my lack of professionalism on wearing our traditional clothing with the style and manner it should be. I still go on learning 'how to elegantly wear a Double Dhoti' like other smart men do, including those younger to me...

This is the third year, am still trying to fix this complex art!

By the way, Nakul bhaiya had put periods to his studies 4 years ago, after two failed attempts to cross over Matric. He is a full blown young man currently, thriving to touch the magical figure, 20. Somi tells that he recently informed Appa about his ambition to become a Rally driver. To get there, firstly, he must be a good engine mechanic and learn driving. Appa arranges with his friend's Speed Motors, the biggest automobile workshop and driving school in our town. Nakul bhaiya got enrolled there last month. He is not a regular there too, but he is a fast learner. Technically brilliant. Way ahead of me. I never match with him in any department, except may be..in a few subjects academically

Somi too had given a Grand Goodbye to her schooling 2 years ago. 'No more academic interests', she boldly declares to Appa in one of her drastic mornings. Appa chased her for a good 10 meters to physically express his strong disapproval. But then, Appa mercifully understands that investing on her studies would be like a criminal wastage of his hard earned revenue

Amma too gives her verdict that Somi has the ability to choose her own paths of life. Somi tragically trips upon the Great Barrier of Matriculation. As a matter of fact, her scores were simply not impressive in all subjects including our very own regional language!

Several times, on days of Maths or English tests, she opens her all-time regional language poetry text book and does meditation for hours together only to smear dust into the onlookers' eyes!

Coming back, there are a handful of new entrants in Matric. The lanky 6-footer Alex. He comes from somewhere in Middle East where his parents are working. He was born and brought up there. Not very conversant with the regional language. Whenever he tried to speak the mother tongue, the whole Class looks at him with simultaneous awe and suppressed fear, for he misses out cardinal alphabets in some technically important words in our very own first-language! Even he himself is not very happy speaking one of the most complicated regional languages spoken in our country. And usually, after his laborious exercise comes to a grinding halt, the whole Class titters, and some gals giggle that extra!

Another not-so-familiar face is Rajan Uthup who joined last year after Christmas Exams. Tall, dark, and sturdy. A migrant to our school from Bhopal

He spoke fluent Hindi, and his regional language proficiency is not too risky, unlike Alex. I remember the day he had joined, one sluggish afternoon Hindi class

Our Hindi teacher, Mr. Damodaran. A thorough gentleman, but looks timid. Comes with a cane, which he scarcely uses. He speaks Hindi throughout the class and has a huge respect for our national language. Never misses the opportunity to show his skill in the language, and engages some of us in Hindi conversation during the class

He tries me once, never makes a second attempt. Obviously, I dash his hopes for ever

Mr. Damodaran cuts jests sometimes

He will start with, 'boys and girls, am going to share something very funny', as though he is going to crack something really humorous worth a hearty laugh!

We lend our optimistic ears, and the joke happens to be outdated and no more in trend often times. Very ordinary, not even qualifies as a banter

Just by the stroke of his luck, we laughed once or twice

When Rajan Uthup arrives, Mr. Damodaran locks him up in a crispy chat. After this, Rajan enters the class when Mr. Damodran makes a brief introduction of Rajan in Hindi. He further asks some out of the box questions to Rajan and translates the same to the class in Hindi itself. I wonder, why at all he makes such a witty attempt at the first place when he knows that it's not a Hindi medium class!

Apart from Alex and Rajan, there're some other giants in our class. One Garry Kurien, Robert D'Souza, and Mahesh. They all form a team. We call it 'Giants Club' in symphony with The Lions Club, which is a high profile, prominent association in our place. Membership to this club is considered a unique symbol of social status

Robert is a Goan descendant, settled in our state for many generations. A fabulous artist. Extraordinarily talented. He makes a portrait or caricature just like that, during the class when it's on. Truly gifted!

Garry stutters during English classes only. No stutters whatsoever, dealing with mother tongue or other subjects. A curious and interesting deficiency in a selective language!

His Maths is horrible. Thought, am the worst in Maths, but to my delightful surprise, I find Garry, any given day, surpasses me scoring below par and makes it to the top spot in reverse!

Mahesh and me are balanced almost, sans, he comes nowhere close to me in English

Alex is generally not good in any subject. He is put up in the school hostel with Rajan and some other guys of my class

Rajan is very good at Track and Field events. Though his core sport is Shot Put, he's an excellent sprinter and a Footballer

He always strikes First place in Shot Put. Champion in 100 and 200 meters dash as well in the School Games

Besides, he's the main stay of our school Relay team. A great finisher taking the last lap

That, Rajan has a huge fan following among the lassies of my class and some other classes is no secret

In studies, there are a few front-runners among girls as well. Rose and Daisy are a cut above the rest

Another very notable guy in the class is Terry. He fairs kay in studies too, not in the top bracket, but may be, in top 10 roughly. This fair and tall cute guy has been with me since, I think, from Class VII or so. Nice and well behaved. His parents too are in Gulf. Another hosteller. He is cool and different from others. Speaks less and looks fresh always. He is Teachers' Ladla. Fairly good at sprint events. Plays Football, I think, he is a midfielder. Terry is an amazing goalkeeper as well

It's still fresh in my memories, during Interschool sports and games, our School Team reached finals by default exactly the same way as India reached Prudential World Cup Cricket finals in 1983...against all odds!

In the final match, we trapped the high profile Sacred Heart Team in a goalless draw till the final whistle. As it's a championship match, the match goes to extra time. Extra 20 minutes too doesn't produce a result. Ultimately, it's Tiebreaker time. The batch of infamous cheer crowd representing our school is hauling and shouting sitting at the cemented gallery seats at the famous Nehru Stadium, for we exactly don't know how to behave as good spectators during a match. We are at the edge of our seats..

The opponent goalkeeper concedes 3 goals and our Terry the 'Dasayev' concedes only 2. What a moment it is! He is lifted on shoulders by other team mates. Having taken the tiebreaker blows, his nose was swollen up the next day morning

Our Headmaster, Mr. Mathews promptly grants him leave during the first session with attendance. What an Impeccable style of rewarding a sportsman for his wonderful contribution in making the school proud!

Overall, Byju is the class toper in studies. He's nothing but an adept in all subjects. Our headmaster predicts, he should be in top 10 rankings in the upcoming State Board Examinations

We've some fascinating teaching staff as well. Our new Headmaster, Mr. Mathews is a seasoned professional. He takes Physics for us. A very strict disciplinarian. Recently, gets transferred to our school aptly replacing Ms. Agnes

Chemistry is dealt with by Ms. Suzzane. Simply walks in with a chalk piece and duster. Kick starts the topic without ignition, and the next 1 hour? Chemical formulae and vigorous reactions engulfing us without a single minute break! Having in-depth knowledge in the subject and English vocabulary, her fluency is as fast as the bullets fired out of a cannon!

Ms. Suzzane is my neighbour, so, even if my mind is wandering somewhere, I pretend to be keenly attentive

English teacher is Ms. Miranda, another neighbourhood teacher

I must say, though neighbourhood teachers are generally feel-good factors, it can sometimes cause hindrance, bring you embarrassing situations when you are their student and don't perform up to their expectations

All are involved in serious studies, for this year is the turning point in our career

'Performance in Matric decides your future. This is your acid test', Appa's daily warning

'Don't waste time. Study well. Don't become like me', Nakul bhaiya

Can Somi be far behind? 'If you simply play around and skip studies, I will inform Amma'. Stern warning from the one who miserably failed to safely cross over the fence 2years ago!

No cautionary words from Granny. She barely knows what a Matric exam is all about!

Granny still pampers me. She hasn't deprived me of that luxury though am no more a kid

'You shall ever remain my prettiest small little toddler', Granny says

Her words remain the only charm in my life

One Monday morning, Ms. Miranda in the class

<u>Topic</u>: Marmaduke, the tortoise and Johnny, the rabbit. The classic race in progress in the class

'Johnny challenges Marmaduke. But then, the clever Marmaduke hatches a brilliant idea to counter Johnny's pace and how to win the race', explains Ms. Miranda

Ms. Miranda is a peculiar type. She enacts expressions and mannerisms of the casts and makes a sudden entry into the character to bring in originality to the audience. But, she is basically a serious person and her body language normally doesn't perfectly synch with the character. It's a terrible mismatch. This is the only lighter part of her nature; otherwise, she's nothing but Lady Gabbar!

She finishes off the chapter and looks around searching for preys to bomb with questions

'Yes Sanju, what's the plan of Marmaduke to defeat Johnny in the race'? Half a chock piece lands straight on my forehead, falls down and cracks, missile from Ms. Miranda

I spring up and stare at her trying to frame up something, but fail

Ms. Miranda glares at me as though she has never seen me before

'I want you to reproduce the whole story in the class tomorrow without the help of your text book. If you miss one word, I will ask Sulochana to stop sending you to my school', warning from Ms. Miranda

She means it, am sure. She did some damages in the past

Next day, first period, English

Ms. Miranda stands in the middle of the class like the Referee in a Boxing ring

'Sanju, get up. Carry on. No compromise on vocabulary, start', Ms. Miranda

I get up slowly having already resigned to my fate, wearing a loser's impression in my body language

'C'mon you filthy trash'. 'What the heck is in your mouth, huh'? Ms. Miranda loses her temperament

'Marmaduke and Johnny....' that's all I could utter. No furtherance, frozen tongue

It's in stark contrast with my normal performance in the subject; Ms. Miranda just can't take that

'What the heck? Marmaduke and Johnny got married and had babies? Absolute contemptuous disregard to my efforts for you cartoons', Ms. Miranda

I still fumble. Something strange forbids me speak out

No, I must show how tenacious a student am. I mobilize all my courage. Turn my neck and glance at the girls...

Am going to meet with my Waterloo today!

By now, Ms. Miranda gives up on me. 'Next week is the class test. I want you to come first Sanju. If you're not making it, I will chop your tongue off. Won't speak again', Ms. Miranda boils up

Oh, my God! I get a short-term reprieve. I let out a sigh

To score better than Byju will be really tough. A Herculean task. But he too knows that I can be the dark horse in a race. I must take out something from the top drawers to make the cut

I make a word of honour to myself

Late in the evening, while serving me Black coffee and Dhal vadai, Amma corners me. She's just back from Kanjikuzhy. Ms. Miranda and Ms. Suzzane reside on the way, hardly half kilometre from our house

'I met your English teacher, Ms. Miranda on my way back. She was strolling in front of her house'

'huh'? I respond calmly. Am sure, Ms. Miranda did the trick

'Teacher had something to tell me about you'

'What'?

'Both good and bad'

'What exactly'? Am not much interested

Per Ms. Miranda, 'Sanju has the potential, but is not performing. He must prove his worth. Am not going to spare him if he doesn't come first in the forthcoming class test. He is lost in the class, I notice'

Amma and me had a mild conversation today after a long time. We don't speak much

Am keeping myself at bay from her since long. Am not very keen to converse with any..

'Am not sure about other subjects. But I'll not disappoint myself in her subject. Let alone Ms. Miranda or anyone else', my firm reply

Expression on her face shows that she is convinced with my response. She looks at me having concluded the conversation

Our tete-a-tete is winded up..

Chapter 18

Amma, Nakul bhaiya, and Somi make a strong team on one side. I often literally feel the existence of a median bifurcating me from the trio spiritually and physically. I spend major part of my free time with Granny. That's emotionally productive. To me, that's all I need!

Not glued much with my friend circle either

I feel the pain of getting detached from Nakul bhaiya and Somi. Amma realizes it, but no change. I believe every mother should have a noble heart when it comes to sharing of love and affection among her children. Here, Amma fails the golden principles that govern the mother – child relationship

Long ago, she showed me the ignominious exit door out of her heart too severe for a young boy to contain. Unbecoming of a mother who is supposed to have true virtues. The physical and emotional trauma I still face at her hands leaves me devastated. These scars shall never ever go away with times. Definitely not!

'Today is the English class test', while going to school, I strike a conversation with Vibha

We haven't been in talking terms since quite some time. I picked up a fight one day evening. In fact, I mocked at her pulling her pony tail, that's her status symbol, rather, any girl's proud asset

'It's dog's tail, and it stands testimony to your shape. How funny it looks', I start pull her hair again

Honestly, she never gets into an unpleasant argument with me whatsoever maybe the situation

'Can't you feel my pain, huh? She pleads angrily but still trying to be as soft as she can

'How can I feel your pain'? Am in no mood to surrender

'Your acts are rebellious. Not for nothing that your Amma lashes you. You're really bad. I hate you Sanju and never cross my path', she dislodges herself from me and walks away back home lonely..

None other than Vibha is justifying Amma's crude ways of dealing with a tender heart, hurts me a lot

Doesn't she have a soft spot for me?

Am I not her good friend? Or Am I only her guide or a companion to fetch her to school and back?

If my Amma is so good, then I should be really bad, as she says. There're too many questions now bothering me

What she said is still ringing in my ears even after weeks. 'I hate you and never cross my path'

Kay, I'll never cross your path. But I shouldn't have taken her seriously. I took it a little too far needlessly, than I ever wanted it to be

A fortnight later, Vibha tries to appease me several times. Accedes to many of my demands, like carrying my notes, Tiffin box, pushing me from the rear with her head while ascending tough roads..

She even gives me a 50paisa coin as monetary compensation. I take the coin but don't budge. This amounts to cheating and this time, she fights with me

After this, I avoid her presence. Don't take her to school. That heartrending hiatus is coming to an end today

'Have you prepared well Sanju'? Her voice suddenly pulls me back to present

'Yes Vibha', am trying to be more courteous to her

She twists her neck half way and gives me a look with the corner of her eyes. Her trademark expression. Probably she's greatly astonished seeing my demureness, which is not usual of me

We don't converse much. Long communications lead to long arguments. Just wave each other while I reach my class. I step into my class room, which is on ground floor. Vibha is in the first floor. I get inside my class. Another 10 minutes to go for the first bell. I can have a fast revision. I open the text book and attempt a last-minute glance of the entire story of Marmaduke and Johnny

'Hey you', Mahesh taps me from behind. He's my random friend in the class

'Hey you', I reciprocate

'What's up man? Have you prepared enough for the test'?

'Well...Fifty-Fifty

'You are pushed to the wall. You must make the cut Sanju'

'I wouldn't leave any stone unturned to make it Mahesh. Ms. Miranda challenged me and gave ultimatum, and the whole Class witnessed it. I accept the challenge with open arms'; I give a soft smile while delivering the last sentence

'Alright pal', Mahesh walks to his seat

I dig my eyes into the text book again

'Good Morning Teacher', chorus from the whole Class. Am shocked to see Ms. Miranda right in front of me

'Good Morning Teacher', I independently wish her

She looks slightly embarrassed for finding me absent minded, but elegantly nods her head

After recording attendance, Ms. Miranda distributes answer sheets to all

It's her style. She brings answer sheets for students while other teachers ask students to bring their own. Paper distribution is over and then she makes an inspection round between the benches, while scrutinizing the books of repeat offenders do cheating. She gets back to the middle

'Class, one single piece of task. Reproduce the story of Marmaduke and Johnny in your own words and phrases in 30 minutes. I don't want text book language. No joker will steal word or phrase from the other joker'

'C'mon, pen in your hand, here we go', Ms. Miranda

I take another couple of minutes before I lock the pen between my fingers. It has been my methodology; spend 2 or 3 minutes to sum up everything in mind just before pen it down. It's my way of igniting the natural flow of words to the nib of my Bismi fountain pen filled with Chelpark ink

Ms. Miranda observes my body language from a distance. I can see her movements as well. She looks at me. It serves like a reprimand as I've not started yet..

Eventually, I give a jump-start. I tend to be a little poetic and flashy in oral or written. Decorate the end product with words and idioms which are uncommonly used, but might have been used in the past by some of the teachers during a contextual learning process or I perceived it from a news paper or magazine article. It has been a 25-minute exertion since I clipped my pen between my fingers. My final product is ready for submission

The day has not been much eventful, thereafter

Me and Vibha take a slow walk back home in the evening

'How was the test Sanju. You'll make it to the top, huh'? Vibha

'Ms. Miranda seems annoyed with me. No idea what's she occupied with', I said

While walking down, I notice that Vibha is silent. No clues. May be, she has some girlish blues, which she may not like to share with me

'What Vibha'? Am unable to contain her silence, for she chats like a Cricket usually

She doesn't seem to be in gelling up lately. I feel it, and it's disturbing

'Nothing Sanju. Am thinking, this is our last year in the school, and what from next year; rather what's in store for us after Matric exam'? Vibha looks bothered

Oh! That's her worry. Same thought has been haunting me too since quite a while. I've no answer

I look down and continue the walk without a word. In fact, the decisiveness follows after the Matric exam, has been bothering me since the start of this year

It's filled with nostalgic moments from the past

Am sure, we'll part ways to different colleges though we may still remain friends in all it's probabilities. May get to see by chance, at the mercy of Amma. If she doesn't mind me dropping in at hers, I too can have a glance in a flash at her. My thoughts are going wild

Losing things closer to my heart has become regular with me. It seems, The Almighty God likes to pick me selectively and deprive me of all my dear things and loved ones

God gives me struggle only to propel me to newer enchanting heights. Says my new-found Hope!

'Hey Sanju, see you tomorrow. I shall wait for you. Don't fool me, kay'? She suddenly stirs up my thoughts

'Bye, I won't miss to take you along'. Am I mysteriously sarcastic within?!

She turns back, gives a gorgeous smile and runs inside

Wow! I can have a dream night today with snowy white angels with beautiful wings, twinkling starry eyes, and windblown curly hairs!

Alas! Tomorrow is a public holiday. Again, no school, no Vibha

Ms. Miranda might correct the answer sheets tomorrow and bring it the day after

After evening bath, I inspect Granny's tongue, epiglottis, eyes, nose, and ear wax. I do this fortnightly after she fell sick last time

Thank God! She seems hale and hearty sans some degenerative changes for her old age. Voice is normal. Gaits, nothing to worry much. Overall fine, except for general weakness and degenerative changes..

The holiday passes. Next day. Am excited to reach school. I drag Vibha not caring much for her small little tender feet

The whole Class is holding breath. The aura and hype surrounding the glamorous foreign language among Indians is very difficult to be expressed in words

Trrinnnngg! Here goes the second bell. Ms. Miranda will come any time soon

Here, Ms. Miranda appears. She has the answer sheets held in her left fist bundled and tagged crossword with the typical white thread

I've butterflies in my stomach and I feel it from bottom to top. Will I score the highest?

Eventually, it comes as a bolt from the blue. Gifting me the most blissful moments of my student life this far..

Ms. Miranda minces no words, 'Sanju comes first. Give him a round of applause, but not aloud'. He scores 18/20'

She then goes on to announce one by one the marks scored by every one

I'm thrilled. My heart expands to the fullest with delight. My eyes filled, though for an amazingly different reason this time. I look up. Thanked Him, for these breathtakingly adorable moments. At last, I prove my mettle. Truly Red-letter moments. I shall ever keep these dream-like droplets of memories of this class and Ms. Miranda forever close to my heart and soul

It takes some seconds for me to ascertain that it's not illusion!

Byju, the genius makes a close second and Rose comes surprisingly third with a difference of 2 and 4 marks each

'Bring me chocolates tomorrow'. Ms. Miranda reminds me before leaving the class

Am in Cloud-9. Begins here, the phenomenal transformation of a docile adolescent boy. This day's going to turn me around for all the goodness!

Evening. I lock my fingers with Vibha's. Finger-lock of Kabbady players. Bend my fingers and make a strong fist with her fingers interlocked inside mine

I promise to Vibha, never to be cross with her ever again

Her round face shines. I see immeasurable happiness right under her wet nose tip

Am not quite certain, whether I'll foster close and nurturing relationship with Vibha in future...

Every day at night before my eyes retire to sleep, I struggle to give a name to our bond. At last, I only understand one thing...that it's strong and deep rooted

The heartening fact is, she still remains the one and only duck in my pond!

Chapter 19

Half past 6 in the evening. I sit quietly to pen down a letter to Joyce. I'll send it across with Jis

I heard from Granny that my youngest aunt has come with her eldest daughter from the next town. They have come to visit the other aunt who lives in our neighbourhood. Aunt and daughter had made a visit to our house before I was back from school

I had met this aunt some time ago when she came to see her sister when she was ailing from Jaundice. I could get to see her daughter. I think, once or so

I write the first word..aunt with her daughter drops in. Amma takes them in. Her daughter sits with me and Granny in the front open space. Since we're the host, I decide to strike some talk

'Hey, what's your name', I said

'Am not your Hey. Address me properly, kay? Am your Nakul bhaiya's age. You know my name is Rajlakshmi. Behave yourself, you chotu', she literally slams the door on my face

'Who are you calling chotu, am much taller than you, and I stand 5 feet 7 inches tall. Recently, I checked my height and weight in our gymnasium, mind you'..I retaliate

'Height, kay.. I may agree, but for heaven sake, please don't brag about your weight'

I immediately realize that she's not an easy guy

She has serious looks. Not in alignment with her probable age. Her eyes are intense and lively behind the thick glass she wears. They resemble beautiful goblets, but gives her a tough look. Her eyes do all the talking. Having a broad forehead, like our KK Road. Overall, she has all the features of a strong girl. She will surely grow up to be fierce with her demands and feelings...

Looking intensely at her face, I wink my eyes for no reason. She returns a perfect graceful look into my eyes...

If I pick up a verbal fight with this her, I will be no match for her

She looks at me curiously. Hopefully, she reads my mind

Let me settle for a meek submission now. Sometimes, the best gain is to lose

Men seldom make passes at girls who wear glasses, the great saying goes...must be for a reason!

Our conversation abruptly ends

She says Bye to Granny and Somi and leaves after a while. 'Tomorrow's is my Birthday. Amma asks me to visit your Narshimhamurthi temple and offer prayers', she says while leaving

'Don't grow up. It's a trap', I tease her from behind

She has paid this visit only to tease my height and weight..I wonder!

I finally, settle down at a corner with writing materials, plain white papers and my favourite fountain pen, which is recently added to my school kit

Dear Joyce,

Hey man, get to know about you from Jis, your brother. Am not sure about the reason for you to leave our school. You know it's rich in heritage with a strong Catholic background. Might be, your present school is far superior to our age old school like some people claim; or might be, you were not comfortable with some of our faculties. Anyways, am happy that you had the choice to move on, unlike me!

Joyce, I couldn't heartily thank you enough for always being my shoulder to cry on whenever I needed someone to empty my basket of emotional stress. Accept my thanks for appreciating all my hard work and sincere efforts to float on the top and survive in this highly competitive and resentful atmosphere, when no one else was. I haven't been always vocal to the extent that others expect me to, even now. I can't shout aloud how much you matter to me. But I must say that am indebted to you for all those nice things you did for me. Be it sharing your answers in Maths or a pat on my shoulder to say, 'take it easy', or when you tried to stop Mr. Lucius Gabriel when he was bashing me with his savage cane. I keep a heartful of gratitude for you my great pal!

You know the sky and the stars and the mighty Mount Himalayas will never cease to exist. Just like that, you will remain friend!

Joyce, I've a serious concern to share. Does the legacy of a crude mother badly influence a boy's psyche and his sensitivity to gel with the opposite sex?

Well, I want you to understand that this 'boy' is none other than me..

What will happen to me as a full-blooded young man whose understanding of a female is determined by the first woman he encountered — a hostile mother?

As you know in tits and bits from what I had shared with you in the past, not a single day passes without being abused by Amma. I've become like the rolling stone in the adage. Just rolling on and on, gathering nothing substantially useful in the long process, which may support my growth as a human being!

It's my deep desire to meet you Joyce. At least once, before I fall and disappear into the treacherous gorge of life

My mind is not in my control anymore. Am losing the reins of targeted direction

Study well and bring name and fame to you and your mother. Try to live up to the legacy of her skills and devotion as a teacher. By the way, she likes me very much Joyce. You know that

Hope, there's light at the end of the tunnel, but there could be an incoming train. The control panel which supervise my emotions, sometimes tells me, like a mysterious voice from heaven that the incoming train has left the station, and I must be ready to welcome it!

Am notoriously mindless. Isn't it Joyce?

This paper goes wet with my teardrops. Can't write anymore. Am in total mess..

I remain, Sanju

Scene transition

Days and weeks pass. Presently, am not very inclined to meet Vibha. My lungs flutter when I see her. Maybe, am not very confident about the promise I had made to her. I can't afford to let go of my promise; it's sure and certain. But then, I can't claim it to be a rock solid commitment either. So, let Vibha carry the hollow belief that I will hold my promise strong and never let it break. Am not going to break her heart again, anyway. And to prepare such a pseudo background, I must keep myself away from Vibha. Nevertheless, I would love Vibha to have complete trust in my promise all the way, may be, till an unknown future date!

I don't know how the time is passing so quick causing so many events in one's life. Some significant, some having no much significance or relevance in your ongoing life. Some people come in your life uninvited, leave a scratch and moves away without your consent leaving you in embarrassment. While some others make their gracious presence in your life for a while, give you lessons, and when you really get to realize and understand the enslaving sweetness of togetherness, they simply walk away leaving behind wistful chronic wounds forever!

I never agree with the traditional theory of 'time eases all things'. Humbug!

Humans undergo various phases in life. Come across different people and share lot of emotional bondage with selective people. And the lessons we receive are also different; sometimes, traumatizing. For, on a certain day, there are these pleasing folks crash open the doors of your heart and stay put in for a while. Some of them make life-changing impacts on your very existence as a person, and on a bad day, simply march away without looking back even once. May be because, there is refurbishing taking place in their lives. It's an automatic process happen in the lives of many people. But for some other, this process never happens in their entire life span. They're captivated inside their soul, and the soul is now worn out and tormented beyond recuperation, in a state of depleted fractions..

And you will never be the same person ever again!

Like the obselete piece of a toy, which was once attractive and indispensable, had been frequently kicked and banged on the floor while playing all these years.. suddenly, is no more attractive and amusing to the kid anymore!

Expectedly on a Tuesday morning, before the first bells goes, Jis comes to me with a half smile and hands me an envelope secured with staples. It's the long-awaited letter from Joyce. I had guessed it seeing Jis walking down to me

I slowly unfurl it during the break after I hastily finished my so-called lunch

Joyce' intellect is of high order. A well-disciplined and updated guy. Upbringing perfectly in line with a stereo-type teacher's child. Not finished, he is now the student of the city's most sought after educational institution!

I am dying to go through his letter. I know, his words are straight from his heart. Beyond all boundaries of my imagination..

Dear Sanju,

Hope, this letter of mine finds you in good spirits. I get to know quite a bit about you from Jis. He brings home a chunk of good news as well as not-so-good news from school. Good and bad mingled

All interesting stuff, except the reports about you. These are sometimes sweet and some other times, sour, I mean, a good fodder for thought, huh?

I think a whole lot about the times when we were together there for those 3 years!

You were always wearing the look of a timid, frail guy with frightened eyes. Always looked troubled in mind. Never made even the least impression that you would make remarkable improvement in studies, let alone kick open big doors of future!

Sanju, no matter what happens, you'll remain my best friend. We find treacherous curvy roads that cause unprecedented disruptions and accidents. There're such bents and turns in real life too capable of altering the paths of our lives. In the long run, I may come across many, and befriend a few out of them, but Sanju, you are unique and humble. There's only one person like you in the whole planet, and that's you yourself man. No one else indeed!

And emotionally, you'll be an integral part of my being!

I gather, you're going through hard times, and whenever you need my help and support, just think of me, and am there just beside, rubbing your shoulders. You bring me so much inspiration every day. You're one of my heroes, for you've made it so far in your gruesome domestic front. I know, you are living dangerously every day fighting your own shadow in the quest of finding equanimity in your life. Sorry, 'your small little insignificant life', in your own words!

My pal, it's foremost and paramount to be 'who you are'. Being 'who you are' is the key to our very own survival with pride, and holding your head high against all odds. Speak what you want to. Call out all your inner power and have the stomach to call a spade a spade. Fight Sanju, fight. Speak out man. Don't shy away from reality even if it bites a little bit

Ya, by the way, I always wanted to remind you one thing. You must've had perceived the courage to stop

Mr. Lucius Gabriel from all those savage attacks on you. He probably thought, you are an orphan and you've none at home to visit the school and confront him on your behalf!

The rigorous brutality you frequently received at his hands is going to be disturbing my conscious in perpetuity. More so, as a collection of recollections soaked in chronic pain!

Mr. Lucius Gabriel was a predator, and you played into his hands like a weak and hapless prey. Being a teacher doesn't mean, he or she enjoys an automatic legal or moral right to treat a minor human being like an inconsequential creature. I seriously doubt whether I would get to see any student being treated like the way you were dealt with, anywhere in my future academics!

He chases you in the class from corner to corner and you run, and intermittently limp for shelter. Many times my eyes filled seeing that pathetic situation. He has always been ferocious! Like a hungry Honey Badger chasing its prey! Never be subdued like you were then in those chilling moments Sanju. Revolt, fight, and win!

Am told that you are showing all-round improvement in leaps and bounds, but that's not enough man. I want you to look up. Don't drop your chin when you feel weary and exhausted. When you are not sure what's the surprise tomorrow, pump up your chest, look beyond your limitations, and think of the best things coming your way. Learn to wonder at small little things and stand agape at amazing happenings around. Believe in yourself. Pat on your own shoulders. Cry out if you're overloaded with feelings of stress and sorrow. Laugh your heart out when you have a good time. Laugh for all those forgotten reasons you felt like you couldn't. And laugh and laugh till it hurts!

I want you to hold on. Have more friends, but be choosy. Vibha is innocent and righteous to be a long-term friend of yours. Again, let someone in other than Vibha if you feel so. Don't fail to listen to your heart. Discuss your dreams and ambitions and fantasies with the most trusted ones. Tell someone, if not Vibha, your biggest fears if you still have any. Tell someone your biggest disappointments. Share with someone your biggest handicaps and weakness, which make you nervous

Don't let go of hope. All you need is, take a deep breath. Grasp somebody's fingers and speak up about your mental fatigue and new starting points. You will meet up with electrifying new beginnings, just like your favourite sunset, which makes the promise of an all new sunrise the next day morning!

Say a firm 'no' to awkward relations and their unwelcome indulgence into your personal arena. Train yourself to conceptualize constant desire to become a better and better individual as days pass by. Hope is real my friend. At times, what you all need is a pretty long walk, your fiery sunsets, a cup of steamy hot Black coffee at a small-time tea shop, and all interesting people who can drive you forward and keep the coal burn till sunrise!

Hope is the quintessential fragment of life. Several of us can't live a life of peace and tranquillity without harbouring hope within ourselves. Life is unpredictable, and so, many unprecedented things appear without invitation. It's hard and quite ugly at times. Things slip out beyond our control. But hope helps us keep the spirit glowing, and further upgrades the provisions of moulding our lives into truly rewarding. Recall when all is lost, hope remains!

When we understand and realize that life is a solid war zone, it's not too bad unlike exteriorly it looks sometimes. Our age is a period of rapid transformation. Take the right track and move straight ahead. One day you'll mesmerizingly surprise yourself!

Hope helps you with divine and invisible strength to sail across a pain, and it also makes the journey to the future easier as well. Let's not worry, for today's bad. Hope keeps us reminding that tomorrow will be better than today. Hope is optimism. When you're hopeful, difficulties of today will soon end. Hope guides us stay positive. If your mind tells you to stay strong on a path and not to lose courage, you will do so. Hope gives tremendous mind power. It generates an aura around you which protects you from all evils, and that's why hope shall ever remain the lifeblood!

Discard all ignoble, unfaithful people from your life. They'll use you for their worldly gains, and one day, will ruin you. Remember one thing, which is of paramount importance in our long journey of simultaneous learning and living. Life doesn't gift you with the people you desire, it gives you the people you need. To provide you support, to hurt you, to torment, and leave you once and for all teary eyed. But in this whirlwind process of affection and dejection, these folks, without their deliberate consent, make you the person you were meant to be..

To conclude, I must say, never be a niggard in seeing dreams. And remember, a dream doesn't become reality at the drop of a hat. It takes sweat, determination, and hard work. But I would still say, no dream is too big. Let others keep barking at you, but you will move on. Challenges shouldn't slow down your pursuance. Instead, it should further kick you forwarding the radical process of rediscovering yourself!

Do get back to me, with all those mind-blowing stuff on you and Vibha

Be the Morpheus, man. Sleep and repeat. And keep your eyes filled with magical dreams!

Stay attached,

I remain, it's your Joyce

I read the letter again and again...till I memorise each and every letter and phrase. It's such an awe- inspiring bit of master class from my Joyce!

Scene transition

Weeks flew by. Matric exams get over. I expect to get through with a First class, but not confident. Vibha says that she would surely pass

If I don't make it in style, Appa's hopes would be dashed. He's already heartbroken with Nakul bhaiya and Somi. And from my personal perspective, it would also mean that I don't have it in me. It would be nothing, but a total collapse of my own self-made calibre..

If that happens, how would I contain it? It's a different story that various phases of life bring different opportunities and situations where we've got to put ourselves out there, keep your fingers crossed and be awaiting. And all opportunities come with a reasonable chance of rejection, and the biting reality that I've experienced rejection plenty times makes me once again apprehensive..

If you search the pages of history, even the most talented people have been rejected in one way or other. Whatsoever, I can't stand it. I will not accept rejection and dejection everywhere. I simply will not. I've had enough!

It's another night. Nothing much changes all these days. Appa's a more punctual daily goer to work, even on festival days. Somi looks aimless as always. Nakul bhaiya, now the tallest in our family, handsomely grownup; brimming with manly features and tons of confidence. Amma still struggles to love me each passing day. And Granny..she looks young and robust!

Lately, I find myself cool and composed. I can feel, my mind and body has undergone a complete overhaul, got rid of all dirt and stain from within, and draped in new outfits and hung in a wardrobe like a brand new hit product in the market!

I'll not resign to my fate so easy. Am not a sitting duck anymore!

Heartful of thanks to Joyce, for giving birth to a new Me from the world of misery I've been attached to. Thanks for sharing the pain behind my tears and thanks for cheering along side as well. You've brought miraculous changes to my attitude and the way I look at things in my surroundings. Your magical words will definitely go a long way in shaping me as an elegant citizen. I can't believe it, but it's true, it's real. Wonders do happen in lives, maybe, in the most unexpected ways and means. But here, I know, it's you Joyce. You've been wonderful all the way!

Staring at the new roof, I firmly shut my weary eyes. My heart is more greedy now, and dying to see those fantasy dreams yet again..one more time..every night!